Seal of Love:
One swipe. One match. What followed was a love steeped in selkie legend and Highland mystery.

Sierra M.KING

ISBN 979-8-9990338-0-2 (Paperback)

ISBN 979-8-9990338-2-6 (Hardback)

ISBN   979-8-9990338-1-9 (eBook)

Published by Dublin Donkey Publishing

DEDICATION

For the people in my life that believed and encouraged me to put pen to paper.

Prologue

Before the sea had names and borders, the selkies swam beneath its surface—seals in the water, humans on land.

With the moon as their witness, they shed their pelts on quiet shores, walking the earth in borrowed forms.

Table of Contents

Chapter 1

Should I be a writer?

Leaning against the sun-warmed bricks of my latest renovation, I peeled off my gloves, sweat trickled down my spine mingling with the humid Florida air. The end of another day, another day of unfulfilled dreams. These days were passing me by like a gust of wind rustling my hair, feels good in the moment but then the work of tidying it up is inevitable. I put all my dreams into nicely decorated corners of my mind to deal with later, telling myself, "This has to stop." Naturally I respond with, "I don't know what you are talking about, I will get to it."

I looked up for a minute only to see, Sharon, my roommate, and best friend, in her signature flowy attire, buzzing up the driveway. Little miss love and peace, will no doubt smack me across the face with kindness and wisdom, remind me there is no such concept as 'we can do that later.' I love this girl in many ways. Our equal ease and acceptance for each other and who we are, has never once been replicated. Some have tried, I have tried, but it ends in ambivalence or an unexpected turn that destroys any trust accumulated. At times I could almost physically see the person, I had slowly leaned on, wanted to believe in, disappointingly crumble to the ground. I am in a clean, clearing of life, at the moment, and it is a peaceful place. It leaves me with space to see there is more. Being a romantic, in love with love has also, unfortunately, given me the burden of instilled sense brought on by life's experiences. I now make sure to peek around the corners, over the hills, not settle for the mask of a beautiful sunset. I call it a burden as, on occasion, I may simply miss what it is, a beautiful sunset. In fact, I know I have done that. Therefore, instead of taking a chance on love and dealing with dismay, regrets and frustration, I turn to ripping moldy, damp wallpaper off hundred-year-old walls. I pick up hammers heavier than myself, find the strength to slam against damp plaster with yellow peeling paint. Pure pleasure of demolishing brick after perfect brick into a pile of dust and rubble, creating space and clearing and light. So simple to transform a solid divider into my elation and euphoria. If only life was so easy.

Sharon's timing is uncanny—like she has GPS tracking on my existential crises. We meet by the worn wooden bench, the one that's become my unofficial office chair. I sit and watch while she unpacks a picnic and chatters on about yoga retreats the art of finding balance in a handstand, she takes quick glances up at my face. I lose my appetite; I know what's coming. Sensing my mood is restless, she will, no doubt, squeeze my hand, look into my eyes and I will either cry or tell her to shut up. I know it's coming...

"There is something going on with you, you seem, a little more… distracted than normal?"

Here we go, "What do you mean, 'than normal?'" My laugh at her honesty is also a tactic to hide my dismay.

She ponders, "I don't know, I have noticed you're not as excited about your projects lately." She gestures behind us at the almost finished house. "Usually at this stage you are feeling relaxed, fulfilled. I don't see that in you now."

I nod and concede, "I know, it's starting to feel like a 'job.' I was wondering what the picnic occasion was about. What gave it away?"

It's funny isn't it, how the heart can yearn for the very things that make your palms sweat and your throat close up? Sharon stopped what she was doing and lifted her head, "You gave it away, you never want to go out with me and Dan anymore and you have your nose in a book or sleeping when you're not working. It's pretty obvious you need re programming and probably a good kick up the ass."

The world needs more Sharons. "I'm fine, really I am, I've just been trying to focus down on what's next, and the revelation is taking a bit longer than I thought, that's all."

"So... what is it, what's going on?"

"Probably has something to do with all my dreams reaching out and demanding I partake. All of them at once. What is that, is that normal?"

"Only if you're lucky, most people don't let their dreams get that close. The general population bury their heads in work or life and completely ignore what would make them happy. Trust me, I know, I see 90% of them at my studio." Sharon bites down on her cheese, apple, and cracker combo.

I assemble my own perfect trio snack, and suggest, "So you know what they are, right, my dreams?"

"Of course, let's see; dog trainer, farmer, horse owner, sail away, and someone to do all that with." Sharon smirks as I gag on my hors-d'oeuvres laughing.

"Farmer? When did I say I wanted to be a farmer?"

"I don't know, but there was a time you were going to buy a farm when you grew up. It may have been put on the back of the pile after you worked on your aunt's dairy farm that summer."

"Oh yes, Jersey Cows. I had never seen so much shit in one place. Yeah, I remember now. Okay so my present daydreams are sail, write and a boyfriend who is happy, easy going, brainy and thinks I am the best thing that ever happened to him. Wouldn't it be amazing to feel so comfortable with someone that you can't wait to spend months at a time, out in the open sea on a 500 sq ft boat? The whole time in a constant flow of excitement, boredom, danger and tension?"

Sharon nods her head in contemplation. "Well, hmmm maybe. Let's just say this is your dream not mine."

I laugh and say, "Pure romance…" I sighed "And you know what, I really do think it's possible."

"Yep, it would also help if you knew how to sail, of course."

"Oh, well yes sure, that's a minor setback. The other thing is writing, writing for hours until my eyes can't stay open. What do you think, should I write an autobiography or maybe fiction, more freeing don't you think? I could always write on the boat actually."

I can see Sharon's head starting to spin.

"Okay, okay girl, hold on a second." She puts her hands up, looks at me and we both burst out laughing. "I knew something was up with you but didn't realize it was quite this intense. So, I think you should start with dating; I have been saying that to you for a while."

My head involuntarily throws back, "Noooo, ugh. That's the part I hate. I just want him to appear," I whine

Sharon states, in that voice I recognize. "Eilish, its time, come on you know it is. You want this sailing dream to become reality, but you keep it safely locked away like it will be figured out by someone one day, presented to you on a platter, not gonna happen. You must be the one to make it happen."

I look at her, while processing her words. "Fine, fine I will sign up when I get home, can't wait to respond to, 'How was your day?' a hundred times. But hey maybe my elusive love is out there. Most likely not, but I will do it, okay."

It's not settled yet, here comes the second verse. Sharon continues,

"So that takes care of the romance and adventure what about writing?" She pauses, "That's an easy one, it's all down to you, no one else. Not much stopping you there except your brain. Although I do get that the brain can be pretty fierce at times."

"Exactly!" Finally, I get a reprieve of Sharon's goal setting. Not for long.

She continues, "Like, just sit down and type Eilish, it will come out, I know it will. I know you, when you put your heart behind something, it happens. What is holding you back with all this anyway?"

"I don't know. Wish I did, I'm stuck in a funk. I think when this house is on the market, I will be ready to fly, feel clearer."

Sharon responds with a possible final thought. "Yes, well,"

"Yes, I know," I ponder, wondering am I brave enough to follow through.

"Eilish," Nope, wasn't her final thought… "You are one of the bravest, most open caring person I know, why do you think you don't have the courage to do this? It's just down to embracing what's uncomfortable. If you can wear those crazy six-inch heels you can sail a boat, write a few hundred pages."

"Ha, yes but what can I lose if I change my mind about the heels, a cut foot? Not a sense of failure from following a lifelong dream that falls apart. Yes, I fail if I don't do it, but nobody knows that except me. My own private disappointment."

Now it's Sharon's turn to sigh, "Sometimes Eilish I want to just shake you. You are the only one that matters, you have to know that by now."

"Yes," I say, "I know, I know but how I reflect on others is part of my life too. Isn't it part of everyone's?"

"I suppose. Seems to work out for the ones who don't give a fuck though. They just do or go because that's what they feel like doing. They don't care how you judge them and they are doing just fine. Okay so let's finish this life crisis up," Sharon continues, "When you get home, we are going to join groups and apps galore, I will get a start before you get back."

I look at her in love and disgust, "I will stop and get a bottle of wine, maybe two."

She is right of course; I have to do it. I have to join writing groups full of over thinking idiots who think they have something interesting to say. Dig around on my phone for some decent pictures to use for the modern-day mating ritual of superficial, mechanical, virtual hunt for love.

The simple 4pm snack of cut apples, cheese and crackers and a friend who listens, is exactly what I needed but didn't necessarily want. The doors were opened, I didn't cry and only a mild suggestion that she shut up. It must be time to jump after all. Maybe I really am at a place of being truly ready. I am in a good place for sure, finances are under control, no relationship and not in the middle of getting over one. Freeing me up to take a step into dreamland.

Timing in life is more about what we are ready to take into our psyche at that moment rather than being positioned in a perfect location. I suppose, 'right place right time,' does sometimes apply, but for me it was finally being able to see reason where I was once completely blind, I created the right time.

The sun begins its slow descent on the familiar backdrop of the now freshly painted, empty house, it's walls echoing with the past, my favorite time of day in South Florida. It is going to be dark soon and I still had to pull plugs and lock doors.

Very difficult for me to ignore her advice since she had once stood where I was, toes curled over the edge of possibility. Now look at her. It wasn't always easy for Sharon. Her dad was an alcoholic, and her Mum wasn't far behind. She learned to survive out of necessity, thankfully it ended up bringing her on a journey to happiness and success. We don't speak much of her past, I was there, so no need. But she doesn't bring it up around others either. To trade predictability for passion was a life lesson she got down without much choice, not much was predictable in her childhood therefore being predictable was not comfortable as an adult. A secure nine-to-five in exchange for the exhilarating pulse of a yoga studio was bound to evolve, well it was a yoga studio or a lion tamer, either way it was never going to be boring or predictable.

For too long I have considered how my adventure would start, questioning over and again, 'how does one begin?' And there it would pause until the next time I had an empty hour. The hours are passing me by and it's unnerving to think I may never actually pursue something within my reach just because I am too terrified to go for it. Will my new resolve to finally listen to my passion for real companionship, adventure, compatibility, be met with success?

Nodding to myself, understanding my own affirmation was needed. I suppose if I do start with lovely, modern dating where, 'U up?' passed for romance, then, in comparison, putting pen to paper and scribbling stories about mystical underwater realms wouldn't be nearly as daunting. Even buying a sailboat, taking lessons and pushing away to the complete unknown all by myself would be simpler than going on a load of basically blind dates.

With this momentary awakening, I knew I had to take action before it fell asleep.

The last ray of sunlight winked out behind a cloud, and I stood amidst the echo of hammers and saws silenced for the day. It was here, in this skeleton of a foundation that once held so many stories untold and Christmases past, that I finally found sense— I resolved to chart a course through the unexplored depths of my passions. Release the words from the vault of my somewhat broken mind and finally skim across the smooth, silky waters to discover the unknown as the wind carries me around yet another corner of her salty world.

Chapter 2

First date

eft, left, left—ah, another picture with no shirt in front of the bathroom mirror. The profiles flickered past like a deck of cards dealt by a Vegas veteran. My thumb was starting to cramp, a sure sign I'd been at this for far too long. But the optimist in me, that wee voice whispering, "keep goin," wanted to believe Mr. Right—was just a swipe away.

'Love the ocean and being outside.' Read the headline on a new profile. 'Brian', there he was, all tousled light brown hair and a grin that projected warmth. I lingered on his image, my thumb hovering in hesitation.

'Passionate about creating a greener planet,' his bio declared. Well, Brian, you had me at 'greener'. My own house renovations always leaned towards the eco-friendly, and here was a bloke who probably wouldn't scoff at my composting habits or rainwater collection system. I got a tiny bit excited; I have learned expectations were not only heart breaking but a total waste of time but the potential of shared interests, and the hope of a unified yet unspoken language of just giving a fuck about what happens around us, was very rare.

I scrolled through his photos—laughter with mates, a picture of him grinning from ear to ear while he sat on the edge of the boat fully equipped with all his dive gear, ready to fall backwards into the deep unknown. My smile mirrored his.

"Swipe right for sustainability," I chuckled under my breath, a private joke between me and whoever was programming the universe's sense of irony today. My thumb made its decision, swiping right. "Matched!" the app chimed, and I couldn't help but feel like I'd just won a small victory against the odds of modern love. It was silly, really, how a simple digital affirmation could set my heart aflutter. "Brian," I tested his name on my tongue, his profile said he was from Scotland. His environmental ethos drew me in, well that, and how hot he was of course. Both of us living away from family and culture, having that distance from home would bring us closer and gave us a big commonality. It opened the possibility of conversations filled with ease.

"Now, Eilish, let's see what kind of trouble this creates." I mused aloud, leaning back against the couch cushions. The uncertainty of this new connection was thrilling, yet terrifying—start of my dives into unknown waters.

The screen blinked with our match, an invitation to start chatting. My fingers paused over the keyboard, the familiar dance of hesitation and desire tangling up inside me. The app, a modern-day Cupid, seemed to smirk from its pixelated perch, as if saying, "Go on, take the leap, may as well, plenty more waiting for ya when I see you back on here in a week or so." Evil, yet had heavenly potential, app.

Hey Brian, I see we both have a soft spot for the ocean, I typed, my message starting off what could be nothing or who knows, between us. I hit send.

Seems we have more in common than just our love for the briny deep, don't we lass? came his swift reply. Finally, not a generic response of 'How was your day?' I could hear a hint of Scottish lilt through his text—a dash of charm that made me smile.

`Is that so?` I typed back, my curiosity piqued as I imagined him on the other side of this conversation, perhaps with a cuppa tea in hand.

`Aye. We both left our homes behind in search of who knows what lol,` he said.

`Ahhh, yes indeed we did, and what did you find?` I asked.

There was a pause before I saw the dots of incoming, `Ever heard of the coral restoration project off Key Largo? I'm down in the Keys now, come back home tomorrow.` He sent a photo of some vibrant corals and some bleached out ones made sick from the water temperature rising.

Ah, that's brilliant! My heart skipped a beat, not only at the shared interest but also because he was in the trenches, sleeves rolled up and heart invested.

My phone buzzed again with his next message. `What about you? Where did your adventure bring you?`

`Restoring older homes,` I responded, `giving them new life while they in turn give me cuts and electric shocks.`

`Well let's hope there is a payday at the end of it all, at least enough to pay for the medical bills.` He typed; I smiled.

`Yes, sometimes even enough left over to feed the dog,` I replied, and to think I was about to call it a night before this ocean man brought me to a halt.

As I typed my response, the corner of my mouth quirking upwards. My fingers typed without instruction just thoughts to page. `So, Brian, tell me more about this love affair with the ocean.`

`Love affair that never ends,` came his swift response. `And you, restoring homes? —Tell me more.`

`It's a living,` I respond. `Just so happens I love every bit of it, wounds and all, so I'm very lucky.` I want to go on, but I feel this is too soon to let him into the back of my thoughts. Warmth spreads through me as I hold myself back from blabbering on and on. I typed, Preserving the past for the future almost feels like threading needles in a timeline.

Interesting way to put it. I'm more of a diving headfirst into the waves' sort of chap.

Sounds reckless, I was finding myself more engaged than I'd been in ages.

It can be but I'm pretty good at taking all relevant precautions, he countered. How do you like it here in Florida, after Ireland?

I like it, what's not to like? I mean, this is a personal objective since I love the ocean. There's a lot to be said about the warm water, boating and the potential to sail away even if I don't know how to sail. I hit send.

typing dots.

Ha ha well I would happily teach you to sail. he wrote back.

So you say, I can be pretty stubborn, I answered, a smile playing on my lips.

For the first time in a long while, the uncertainty that often clouded my adventures in modern dating seemed to lift, replaced by a flicker of genuine curiosity. Who was this Brian fella?

I leaned back, the phone warm in my hand. Maybe, this was the start of a story worth diving into. That's a big 'maybe,' I don't trust any of them, even the Scotts. Like I said, expectations are the enemy.

This story, which includes both love and the vast ocean, marks the start of my writing journey. It began with an app, a dating app full of hope and disappointment. Then using a mix of memories and current events, I crafted a scenario based on my personal experiences, sprinkled with wishes and creative ideas. I hope you enjoy it.

~

Is that too much for coffee? Eilish's duvet is buried under fashion ideas from her closet. Okay, this is perfect, a little sexy but not trying too hard. Landing that combo of casual but hot is an acquired formula. As I bound down the stairs, my dog, six inches ahead, runs for his lead, I remember… the dog has to be walked.

I don't usually dress up, my average attire is yoga pants and some sort of sun shirt. If I go to a hair appointment or perhaps a doctor's appointment, I throw on some clothes that exist on a hanger rather than something stuffed in a drawer. I do this to see how they feel or look in the outside world, a different environment. Do they elevate my swagger when I see myself in foreign mirrors, am I pleasantly surprised? Do they bring an essence of joy I didn't have in my yoga pants and sun-shirt? If the answer is yes, I keep that outfit. This system works for me, many times I have donated an outfit because of it.

Dog is walked, shoes are picked, stuff my phone in my black leather, thrift store bag, keys, water, always water. I better pee first, drop all the stuff to pee, then start over but an easy collective grab this time. No need for GPS, I know this place.

Man, it is hot outside, a summer day in West Palm Beach, Florida, takes about ten years to get used to and even then, it's a shocker anytime between 10am and 6pm. After 7pm it's the most stunning place I have ever experienced. The sunsets are reddish-orange with sweeping soft clouds, humidity lifts just a tiny bit but enough to appreciate the earth has finally moved away from the sun, not all the way but now the elements allow me to strip down to fully exposed skin without the worry of a scalding, ultraviolet, possible death sentence. Hence my usual garb of yoga pants and SPF 50 shirt during the day.

I am about ten minutes from our agreed coffee joint. I text and let him know my estimated arrival. I like to be a bit late.

He texts back, `I'm here, blue shirt and jeans, see you inside`. My adrenaline is kicking in, even though we have talked and texted quite a bit, meeting in person is exciting, some meetings more than others, I was anxious to see how this one went. I opened the door to a half empty coffee place, the wafting smell of fresh coffee hits my already heightened senses, I scan the white light room over the echo of wooden table legs on tile floor, loud, grinding, screeching coffee machines, and music in the background. There he is, looking at me, grinning, not trying to get my attention, just peeking out from behind a large woman in the coffee line. Mr. cool, no sign of adrenalin on him, I had the same grin. He looked very much like his picture; he was definitely hot. Seems like we both like what we see. I walked over to him, smiling at him smiling. We gesture to hug while questioning at the same time. We quickly hug and say, 'hi.' It was long enough to feel his strength and soak in his smell. That moment can be awkward but not this time. He asked me what I wanted and then he ordered mine along with his.

Now that's a very normal, simple gesture but one I have only recently come to terms with. In the past I would make it a point to cut him off while he was ordering and put the order in myself. I understand why I had the need to do that then but now I am more secure in my being that I don't feel threatened by a man ordering for me. If he wants to order two drinks instead of just his, please be my guest. Another issue I have on a first date is do I pay or assume he will pay. At this stage of dating, I am so used to the guy paying I would also probably question if he didn't. It's a tough one, only because him paying can be associated with control rather than a kind gesture. Sometimes it is control but most times it is him being a man wanting to provide and not necessarily him assuming I am not capable. It has balanced out in the past with the man paying for certain stuff and I pay for certain stuff. I pay for groceries or toilet paper. In a sense we are taking on very traditional rolls but these days it's a choice. I like the feeling of being taken care of and since most men don't have the emotional health or understanding of how to express that with words or gentle touches, they show in financial gestures or acts of service. It would be nice to have both, but it hasn't come into my life yet. I don't think this will be the guy to change that. That's okay, as long as we have long hugs, sexual chemistry, communication, things in common, okay I will stop. Did I mention I am allergic to expectations, nevertheless I do find myself scratching at them at times.

I knew his parents were Scottish and he spent the first 19yrs of his life in Scotland, much like me and my time in Dublin. Like I said, it does help with the fluency of communication when there is a direct European connection. We stand waiting for our coffee, grateful for all the background noise to block out our silence. Neither of us try to converse, it's too loud, other people within ears distance also waiting for their coffee. Those first few sentences are tough. We don't know each other, who knows what the responses will be. I like to wait until we sit and are in a relatively private spot, seems like he does too. I shift weight on my feet, look around and finally, 'Eli' soy decafe café latte?' 'Brian, cafe latte?' They always mess up my name, we collect the coffees, look at each other and then at the outside seating area, I nod. Outside, even in this heat, is better than the café's orchestra inside. He pushes the door, I look up, smile then walk to a quiet corner with an umbrella and table for two, he sits across from me. This is the moment that reveals if coffee was the right choice, or dinner would have been fine. It usually doesn't take long to figure out, about 5 minutes. I should have got an iced drink. I have fair skin; I feel a little flushed. I have a good chance to really take him in, okay he is out of my league there is no way this is going to happen. I think he is probably happy this is just coffee. He is eight years younger for starters, thick blondish, brownish, surfer type hair, shoulders I could rest not just my head but my whole body. He is in shape, not too much. I say, "So we made it," as I try to read what's in his thoughts.

"We did, and very happy we did, I have been looking forward to this since our first texting." He responds.

Well, well this is interesting, okay I can relax now. I say, "Me too." He sits back in the normal size chair that now seems small to his 6'3 stature. He says, "loved your profile, the honesty behind it, especially where you say, 'I can be a real pain and a 'know it all' so matches beware."

I laugh, "Yes that's me, a pain in the ass." I explain, "I was attempting to attract funny, honest, strong men. At least if the guy knows up front I have, let's say, stubborn tendencies, he is prepared. I'm actually not sure what I was getting at there, maybe a type of pre-self-sabotage?"

He lightly laughs. "Well not sure, I will use my right to remain silent on that one. But yes, all for honesty and communication."

Hmmm not only does he know what I'm on about, but he also memorized a line from my profile! Must be the Scottish roots peeking out. Not sure an American would have quite got my sense of humor on that one. I think I was being a little rebellious or maybe I wrote with the intention of take me or leave me. The human mind, a constant source of confusion.

I said, "I love that you like to sail, and how quickly you committed to teaching me," We both chuckle. "You don't have a long rambling profile like mine, so I have limited info on you, which is fine, one rambler is enough."

He sat forward and told me he will tell all now, whatever I want to know.

I said, "Okay."

He told me about a couple of his sailing adventures, where his mom and dad are from in Scotland, how they took him sailing all around Europe when he was just 4yrs old. His parents are from a small town called Tobermory on the Isle of Mull, an island off the west coast of Scotland.

I googled Tobermory when I got home. It is a gorgeous town, but I get it, me being from Dublin, which is New York City compared to Tobermory, I understand fully why he wanted to seek out the unknown. Not that America is unknown per se, we saw plenty on the T.V growing up, but it's definitely got a lot of unknown features in real life. The size for one, the vastness, way of life, the system, there are a lot of surprises. You feel like you have the hang of it and then, surprise! you are splat in the middle of something much different and unexpected.

A couple of hours went by, the coffees were long gone. I was exhausted, my adrenalin had been up the whole time, I didn't have any left. One on one chat with stakes involved had me drained. Abruptly, an interrupting buzz of Brian's phone shattered our cozy bubble. He glanced at the screen.

"Sorry, I've got to take this, it's my mum," He murmured, a crease of worry etched between his brows as he stepped away.

I sat there, the remnants of our laughter still hanging in the air, now tinged with an undercurrent of unease.

I saw Brian's shoulders tense as he listened intently, his hand running through his sexy hair in a gesture that spelled distress. A chill skittered down my spine despite the Florida sun streaming through the openings in the umbrella.

He returned, the storm in his eyes belying the calmness he tried to project. "Eilish, I'm sorry, but something's come up back home. In Tobermory. It's urgent."

"Is everything okay?" I asked, the question feeling unfitting against the weight of his concealed turmoil.

"Ahy, it's just... family stuff," he said, the Scottish lilt of his voice frayed at the edges. "I need to sort it out."

"Of course," I replied, my heart sinking like a stone in still water. "You have to go, then?"

"Looks like it," He admitted, casting his gaze downward. "I didn't expect to—

"Hey, no explanation needed," I interjected. "Family first, right?"

He nodded, though I could see the reluctance in his eyes matched my own. As quickly as our connection had sparked, it fizzled under the pressure of his impending departure.

"Well, look, we can pick up where we left off when you get back." I said.

"Would you wait for a wandering Scott?" His smile was hesitant, but it reached his eyes, igniting a flicker of hope.

"Depends on the Scott," I teased

Brian stood, his tall frame casting a long shadow over the table. "I'll be in touch, Eilish. Thank you for understanding."

"Safe travels, Brian." My words were genuine, but as he walked away, I couldn't help but wonder if this was just another chapter in the unpredictable saga of my romantic escapades—one that might never find its conclusion.

Chapter 3

Doubt sets in

After a month passed and nothing, I hopped back on the app to 'move on.' Using the term 'move on' in this scenario does seem a bit drastic, I only had one date! Yes, well, there are dates and there are dates. I flicked through the dating app with zombi like swipes. The faces blurred into one another, none sticking long enough to imprint on my memory. Until I came across Dave's profile - tall, dark, and handsome in a familiar, average way. But let's be real, I wasn't looking for a potential match; my mind just needed something to distract it. Weeks had passed since my last date with Brian, and I was trying to move on from that disappointment. Dave and I matched, here we go.

"Could be worse," I murmured to myself as I tapped hi and shoved my phone into the fraying edges of my denim pocket.

This dating scene is weird, flippant. Although the Brian match was particularly peculiar as the connection was absolutely there, I know it was!! Obviously not Eilish.

My drive home that day after the Brian date was full of smiles and thoughts of how he would teach me to sail, my hair in the wind as he held onto that big sailing wheel with one hand and my waist with the other, both of us laughing.

I'm such an idiot. Sometimes it almost felt like something happened to him but then I had to question, was that my mind trying to balance out my loss of expectations, creating mystery where there was none? Sharon watched me go from smiles to confusion to disappointment to forget HIM! And then back to normal. This wasn't the first time she had watched this process, not normally after one date. I have been dumped and been the dumper. In one of my past relationships, right before I was dumped, I had felt everything was dreamy, swimming along, getting better and better but alas, apparently not. He didn't feel like he was ready for a 'relationship,' and boom, that was that. My train of joy stopped and his went in another direction. Sharon was there for that, so she knew my process of evolvement. Of course, being stalked was no picnic. I think it was less stressful for her when I was broken up with. Having a man show up uninvited and not take, 'she is not home,' as the answer he wanted to hear, was no fun either. Luckily, I have known Sharon since first grade, she is as easy-going a person you will ever meet, out of the blue says the most profound statements, funny remarks, has an amazing boyfriend who is just as understanding and easygoing. She is a free spirit, takes on life as it presents, always in a steady stream of calmness. She manages to swim out from under any upheaval unscathed and a stronger swimmer for it. I test the temperature before I jump in, but my thermometer is usually broken, reads warm and ends up being oh so cold. I think too much and then not enough at times. I have always liked to know, 'why?' find the reason, the facts, I blame my journalist father. Questioning is in my DNA. But the trick is to ask the right questions. I ask what I want to hear and ignore areas I should not.

A month later, as I swipe and text, avoid requests to talk on the phone, my mind flips on and off about Brian's mysterious vanishing. Why would someone put on such a performance to someone he had no intention of contacting? Maybe to avoid an awkward goodbye? Didn't want to say, 'Look I like you but I'm just not feeling it,' Come on, my radar can't be that much bent? I agree to meet the Bumble match guy, Dave, why not? I have more time as the house is almost coming to an end, some landscaping still to do, then that's it.

landscaping is my favorite part, if I'm lucky and landscaping falls in winter that is. Summer Florida landscaping is tough. It's a good idea to plan on early morning or evening planting. Basically, you have a choice dawn or dusk mosquitoes or heat stroke. This house was finishing up in the summer but had lots of big trees casting a much welcome shade. First order was to install sprinklers as the sprinkler, the water, is the main character. A Florida garden without water and the show is over. Watching a dry, sixty year old garden come back to life is miraculous. Plants appear I have never seen before; bees and birds show up to a once quiet space now full of nature's noises. I spend a good bit of time at the garden center, wandering, designing in my mind, adding color and quiet shape to different ends of the garden.

So, the meet up with Dave also goes well, actually better than I thought but it's over in 30min and missing the illusive vibe. We hug goodbye. He asks me if I would like to meet again, and I say 'Sure.' as I think about Brian and wish it was him that was asking me. Damn it! Forget Brian! I get out of bed early the next morning, walk the dog, make a smoothie, grab a water bottle and keys, ready to hit the garden nursery. It's never early enough, still a waft of heat as I head out the door, but experience has told me this is nothing, compared to waking up at 8am and getting out the door at 9:30am, nightmare. 7am departure is the trick. The nursery is west of where I live, about forty-five minutes. Not many cars on the road yet, listening to the Howard Stern Show on Sirius radio. I see a white truck driving east, looks like Brian's truck! Whatever, there are tons of those trucks. As it gets closer, I see a shape in the windscreen, I get a good look as he drives past. What the… it can't be, he doesn't live around here, he said he lived further north than me, Jupiter I think he said. Holy crap! It is him. Interesting, so I was wrong. A tiny moment hit me where I wished I was right, and he was almost fatally injured, he would contact me when he recovered. There he was very much alive and not almost dead. Okay, well that was good, now I can stop all thoughts and move on. I can officially affirm he is a dick. I pulled into the nursery, grabbed my sun hat and bag, still questioning what I just saw. They know me here, know to let me wander, do my thing. I like to first walk around to see what they have and then double back putting it all together for the different areas of the garden. I spotted a beautiful plant that I hadn't seen before, while reading the information card I felt a tap on my shoulder, I turn to say, 'it's okay, I'm not ready to decide yet…,' and it's him! He is literally standing right in front of me, and I'm all dressed up in my straw hat and work clothes, great. I was mad, confused and happy. He just stood there watching my brain process, it was a matter of seconds but seemed minutes.

He finally spoke, "I saw your car in my rear-view mirror."

I think to myself, okay so that explains how you are in front of me, but I need quite a bit more explaining than that. I stand there nodding my head as if everything was normal, I say "Okay, but I mean… okay." I realize we had one date and for me to overreact at his disappearance would be unprofessional dating. I react nonchalant as my limited acting chops allow, projecting good to see you, haven't thought about you at all, you're the weird one for doing a U-turn to come see me, mode. He is on to me, he knows.

"Eilish, I am so sorry, the whole thing took longer than I thought… anyway, I just got back last night, I was going to call you today."

I say. "No, no it's fine, they keep you busy there don't they? Really, it's okay, but it's good to see you. listen, I hope everything turned out well." I gesture that I should get on with my important plant picking.

He says, "Okay I will let you go then." He starts to turn and walk away but comes back, "Would you be free tonight?"

I respond, "I can't tonight," I nod my head, not suggesting another night.

He gets the idea and says, "Okay, another time then?"

"Yes," I say, "Another time." I turn away. As I hear the crunch of his feet on the nursery gravel get further away, I am dying inside, what was I supposed to do? 'I was busy at work,' is not an excuse, not in cell phone era. Obviously, he must have been going on other dates, or some girl dumped him, I was second choice. I suppose I will never find out, I was cold and indifferent, so much for communication and honesty. I showed him…I muttered, 'ego is a terrible thing.' How am I supposed to focus on landscaping now, what a pain? I got a few plants but accepted I will have to come back another time.

Chapter 4

Brian is back

The gentle caress of the Floridian sun was a stark contrast to the brisk Scottish air Brian had just left behind. His feet, once accustomed to the solid feel of Tobermory's rugged terrain, now sank into the soft embrace of West Palm Beach's swamp and sandy shores, his two hangouts. It felt good to be back.

"Ye've been away too long," Brian muttered to himself, basked in the light of the setting sun. The beach stretched out before him. He thought of Eilish...*I hadn't realized how much she meant to me. Wild seeing her at the garden center, I knew I blew it, I should have been open and apologized a bit more or at least given some sort of explanation, how do I explain it though. Damn she really seemed like she wasn't interested anymore. I think we were both unprepared. I hope I'm not too late…I would really like to see her again.* A sense of urgency fluttered in his chest. He took out his phone and the screen lit up with Eilish's contact, his thumb hovering over the call button.

He pressed call and waited, the ringtone echoing in his ear like the distant cry of gulls. No answer. *A text then, maybe? Aye, less intrusive.* He thought. He tapped out a message. Sent.

Eilish's POV ~

"Would you look at that sunset?" Dave remarked, his gaze fixed on the horizon where the sky blazed with strokes of orange and pink.

"Stunning," I agreed, but my attention wasn't on the fading light; it was tethered to the vibrating phone in my handbag. I felt a prickle of both disappointment and excitement when I saw a missed call and then texts from Brian. Well, well, well, look at who it is. I swear they always feel when you have finally moved on. I don't think so, he had his chance. Who was I kidding? Dave was nice and everything, but it wasn't there whatever 'it,' is. I was thankful I was out as I probably would have picked up right away and that, as we all know in the first stages of dating, is a faux pas. Yes, I was not being very polite towards Dave in this situation, but the days of being polite at my own expense, are over.

"Everything alright?" Dave asked, his brown eyes peering at me over the rim of his glasses.

"Ah, yeah, just..." I faltered, trying to hide my deceit behind a half-hearted smile. "Just missed calls from a friend. It's nothing."

I tucked the phone back into my bag, trying to shake the feeling of longing that crept up unexpectedly and annoyingly.

"Are you sure?" Dave pressed gently, clearly sensing my distraction as we strolled along the boardwalk.

"Positive," I lied, what else could I say? That the missed connection with Brian felt like a dropped stitch in the fabric of my day?

But it didn't matter, the gap bridged between us was there at the beginning and unfortunately not much Dave could do to change that, not with the squeaky wheel of a Scott rolling around in my head, a canyon widened by a simple, unattended text message.

~

Brian had a nagging thought: *What if she really didn't want to hear from me?*

"Dave, do you ever worry about... I don't know, the world?" I asked abruptly, the question slipping out as we left the boardwalk behind.

"Well, yes of course but," Dave replied, his voice measured, and a little puzzled. "But what can one person do, you know?"

"Yes," I mused. My gaze lingered on the ocean, its surface shimmering under the moonlight, concealing the scars of human neglect beneath. I decided to ignore his response, I mean what do you say to that? Nothing positive on my end.

Another vibration from my purse. I fished out my phone. Brian has done a one eighty, that's for sure. Confusion a twinge of guilt and warmth swirled within me like a hot tub on full power. Why now? Why tonight?

"You can get that if you want, you know." Dave said, catching the flicker of emotion on my face as I slipped the phone back into my purse.

"No, honestly, it's okay, I'm sure it's just some silly gossip." I lied again, forcing a smile. My fingers itched to respond to Brian, to dive into the virtual sea in search of understanding, but instead, I focused on the clink of our glasses and Dave's handsome features as he talked about his day.

The missed connection with Brian cast a shadow over the evening. The longing for that shared spark, that camaraderie of ease and admiration, got to me with each sip of wine.

"Dave, do you ever.."

"Get sand in my shoes?" he interrupted, chuckling as he shook out his loafers. "All the time. It comes with the territory of dating a beach lover."

I laughed—a genuine one this time—at least he was attempting to lighten the mood. But even as we shared a dessert, all I wanted was it to be the last bite so I could finally go home.

Brian, the man I wanted, thought about at least twice a day, had desire to make amends. To reconnect yet there I sat, caught in the ebb and flow of dating uncertainties. I wondered if I could navigate these emotional tides this time without capsizing.

"Let's head back," I suggested eventually, my mind still wading through the missed call and texts of what-ifs. As Dave led us to his car, I wanted to be alone, get home to think. This was our third date, and I knew it would be our last. He was walking me to my front door, or so I thought but then he asked if he could use the bathroom. He casually slipped off his shoes by the door before heading down the hall to the bathroom. It was a simple gesture—one that should have felt intimate or endearing but instead, it stirred in me an unsettling blend of guilt and confusion. I went to the kitchen for a glass of water.

When he came into the kitchen, I put my glass down and walked him to the front door.

"I would love for you to stay for a nightcap but really I'm not feeling all that well." I said, masking my inner conflict with a tone slightly lighter than the muggy evening air.

"Thought I might tuck you in." Dave grinned, oblivious to the tempest brewing within me. "Unless you're kicking me out?"

"Actually, I really am feeling awful," I lied, clasping my hands together as if to wring the truth from them. My voice sounded hollow, even to my own ears. "Maybe it's something I ate."

"Ah, no problem," he said, his brows knitting with concern. "I can stay and take care of you."

"Really, I'd rather just sleep it off." The words slipped out, each one heavier than the last. I could see the disappointment cloud his face, but I was getting a little nervous now as he didn't seem to take the hint. Then a grateful slam of an upstairs door and he knew I wasn't alone. I'm not sure if that was the catalyst to get him out, I hope not. I suppose I will never know.

"Alright, if, you're sure." He leaned in for a kiss that never came; instead, he settled for a brief squeeze of my shoulder before gathering his things.

As the front door clicked shut behind him, I could breathe, enjoy the relief of being home and not have to hide behind the mask of politeness. The faint buzz of my phone. It was Brian—another text. Each notification dragging me closer and sending a flutter of terrifying excitement throughout my being. What he did hurt, I didn't want to go through that again. But this feeling of being connected, was out of my control.

"Right then," I muttered to myself, pulling up the message thread. My thumb hovered over the screen, a digital crossroads where one tap could change everything. A simple `hi` was all I typed. Minimal effort, maximum impact—or so I hoped. 'Hi' was safe, non-committal. It didn't betray the turmoil inside me or the way my heart raced at the thought of hearing his voice again. It was a lifeline tossed into the murky water. "Sent," I whispered, releasing a breath I hadn't realized I'd been holding. Now, it was out there in the void, signaling my willingness to find our way back to each other amidst the uncertainty that kept us apart.

My phone, a traitor to the cause of my feigned indifference, was buzzing against the palm of my hand like it had just sipped a double shot of espresso. I flinched, surprised by the suddenness. But I didn't dare look. Not yet.

I blinked down at the screen and there it was, Brian's name lighting up the pixels with an urgency that felt both alarming and exhilarating.

```
Hey Eilish, I'm so sorry again for disappearing, I've
been tangled up in work, but that's no excuse. Can we talk?
```

A laugh bubbled up from my chest, half amusement, half disbelief. Could it be this simple? I stared at the message as if it might sprout legs and scuttle away, leaving me once again in the land of 'what if.'

"Talk?" I whispered, mocking the casualness of his request. Since our last conversation at the garden center hadn't been loaded with enough unsaid things to fill the hold of a cargo ship, talking was probably a good idea.

But then another text arrived. `I really want to make this right. How about dinner tomorrow night? A chance to clear the air?`

The word 'dinner' hung between us. Brian wanted to meet, not just swap digital apologies but actually sit across from each other. I don't know.

"Clear the air," I mused, tapping my fingers against the edge of the phone. It wasn't just his past indifference that made the atmosphere thick between us—it was also the weight of everything unsaid.

`Sure,` I typed back, my thumb bold where my voice might waver.

The immediate '😄' that pinged back —I couldn't help but smile.

`Okay, brilliant, I look forward to it Eilish` he replied, and I pictured him there, on the other side of the text, flashing a grin as big as mine. Two idiots grinning into space

Shaking my head. It was funny, really, how yet again, a couple of words could hold the promise of a fresh start.

"See you tomorrow, Brian," I murmured to myself, a silent affirmation to keep the nerves at bay. Tomorrow, we'd navigate these waters, hopefully navigate around any possible storms.

~

"Sure, he's kind," I muttered to myself, thinking of Dave's predictability, but the connection simply wasn't there, and no one ever penned sonnets about men who complained about sand between their toes. it kinda freaked me out the way he wouldn't take the hint to leave last night. Dating for a distraction is probably not a good idea. I am less focused on the details; I don't care as much therefore too easy to miss dangerous red flags.

"Right then, dinner it is," I said, finally breaking the stalemate within me. my inability to stay away from the sea—or from those who loved it as much as I did, was a constant in my life. Time for bed, I would sleep well tonight.

I woke up thinking with a simple *yes* and a time, the die was cast. My feelings had shifted since his departure it will be interesting to see where they land tonight.

The restaurant's ambiance was muted, with seashell hues and soft lighting—an attempt at recreating the serenity of the shoreline indoors. Brian was already there, his easy smile stood out in the dim room.

"Hey, Eilish," he half got up from the booth he was sitting at and waved to get my attention. That Scottish tone in his voice wrapping around my name like a warm embrace. There was no awkwardness, only a shared understanding that hung between us, unspoken but palpable.

"Hi, Brian," I replied, sliding into the booth opposite him. "Let me just say it is great to see you and so far, I am happy you were persistent but… what the fuck happened?"

Brian realizing there was no point in using his usual charm to deflect the obvious responded, "Ha, well you don't waste time do ya, look I'm really sorry Eilish, it was work and someday I hope I can give you more information but for now can you please forgive me and I promise in time you will understand."

As I watched Brian go into his short but compounded reason for neglect, I thought, *okay so I'm being a bit dramatic, but it was a crazy strong first date!* I felt stupid, empathetic and understanding all at once. I believed he had good intentions and wasn't just fucking with me. That's all I had, my instincts. They hadn't kicked in too well in the past so let's hope all the buttons were turned on for bullshit detecting this time.

I nodded my head and then looked straight up at him "I accept your apology, and I suggest we leave it in the past."

Brian sat back, through up his arms and said, "Okay then, what are you drinking my fair lady?"

As we delved into discussions about recent clean-up efforts and strategies for growing and replacing coral, the world outside the restaurant's windows seemed to recede. Our conversation ebbed and flowed naturally, punctuated by the clinking of cutlery and the hum of distant chatter.

"Yea, it's nae just about cleaning up what's already there," Brian said passionately, leaning forward. "We need to stop the rubbish at the source."

"Yes," I agreed, feeling a surge of admiration for his conviction. "It's like trying to renovate a house while someone is still living inside breaking things right behind your efforts."

"Exactly! And if we dinnae act now, there'll be more plastic in the sea than fish before we know it," he added quietly, almost as his own inner worry.

"I know," I murmured. "But hey, let's go a little deeper about you, and forget the tragic world we live in, for an hour at least."

"Oh no Lass, that's a lot more dangerous than our crazy world, I would like to know a bit more about you though."

I ponder and look at him, I see now he has a lot heavier and thicker wall to dismantle than I have tackled before.

I tell him about my move to Florida and about Sharon but much like him I was on guard. Although to be fair, I had good reason to be. As the night went on our shared laughter filled the space around us, rekindling our connection. This was the essence of us—our passion for the environment, our laughter amidst the fight. It was as if the ocean itself had conspired to draw us together.

A hint of jasmine from the neighboring gardens. The low hum of conversation formed a soothing backdrop, I was barely aware of the other diners; my focus was entirely on Brian.

"Listen, Eilish, about before..." His voice held a tenderness that made my heart skip, I could feel an apology swimming out of the depths of his being. "I dnnae handle things well, rushing off without proper goodbye. Can ye forgive an eejit like me?"

I took a sip of my wine, letting the rich flavors dance on my tongue as I considered his words. There was something about the remorse in his eyes and facial expressions that wore down my defenses. With a soft exhale, I set my glass down and met his gaze head-on.

Surprised he is bringing it up again but a sense of relief in his continued sincerity.

"Consider yourself forgiven," I replied, feeling the weight of uncertainty lift from my shoulders. There was comfort in this easy banter, a reminder that despite the rude disappearance, there was a vail of light around us worth keeping turned on

"Thank you, lass, truly." He reached across the table, his fingers brushing against mine—a gesture so simple yet laden with intent.

As he brought his hand back to his side of the table, the sounds of the bistro seemed to swell around us, the clatter of dishes and the murmur of conversations resuming their place in my awareness. Within me, there was a newfound harmony—a sense of understanding.

"Another one?" Brian asked, his eyes alight with shared purpose.

"Absolutely," I agreed.

"Tell me about the house you're working on, was that the reason you were at the garden shop place? Oh, you were a little tiffed at me I think." He chuckled, signaling the waiter for another round.

Before I could interrupt him by demanding I had good reason to, he put his hands up and said, "I know, I know I deserved every second of your madness."

I jumped in and said, "Well yes you did, but I wasn't mad, well maybe a little, but mostly confused."

We stopped going back and forth and looked at each other, he asked with a coy quiet smile. "Are you still confused?"

I responded, "I don't think so but you never know, I might start chasing my tail any minute." We laughed.

I had my wall up too and he wasn't getting behind it that easy.

And just at that moment, amid the laughter and restaurant sounds, our evening felt like it took a turn into a place of, 'you never know again.' 'You never know,' that place of possibilities, but of course, walls and expectations are on high alert.

As the conversation continued, the lightness was evident, the ease impossible to ignore.

"I mean, here we are, capable of so much, advancing at rapid speed, but keeping the beach clean seems beyond our grasp, never mind the actual ocean?"

He nodded thoughtfully. "It's daft. But the truth is, every wee bit we do helps. Like your house restorations, it's about taking something neglected and giving it new life, re-using what we can."

"Yes," I agreed. Enjoying the camaraderie and understanding,

"Hope," Brian lifted his glass for a toast, a gentle chuckle accompanying his words. "And maybe, we're not entirely daft for believing in it."

"Hope," I said as we clinked glasses, allowing a small laugh to escape. "But wouldn't it be grand if the world proved us right?"

"Grand indeed," he replied, raising his glass in a silent toast to our mutual agreement of positivity about something that was out of our control.

As we strolled down the moonlit beach after dinner, Brian reached for my hand, feeling the warmth and strength of his hold sent an extra light throughout my being, a light that zinged inside me. This was good, this was really good. Our conversation continued to ebb and flow with the tide. We'd shared laughs and comfortable silences, but the depth of our connection, it just wasn't something I had felt before.

"Ye know," He said thoughtfully, his Scottish brogue curling around his words, "I've always believed the sea holds a bit of magic in her depths."

"Magic?" I echoed, half-teasing, my bare feet sinking slightly into the warm wet sand.

"Exactly," he replied with a playful grin. "It's that kind of wonder that we're fighting for, Eilish. To keep the ocean alive with its mysteries and not just... choked with rubbish."

"What mysteries are we talking about here? You mean like pirate ships and hidden treasure or the science aspect of mystery?" I asked.

He chuckled, "Well yes sure buried treasure is mysterious but I'm talking more about what we don't know. It doesn't make sense that we spend so much time, money and effort on space when we have so much to still uncover about our oceans right here in front of us. But I suppose that's where hope comes in, doesn't it?" He asked, turning to face me. "Without it, what are we even doing here?"

"True," I admitted, feeling the weight of his gaze like an anchor grounding me. "And hope has this funny way of turning into action when you least expect it."

He stopped walking, gave me a slight pull towards him and kissed me. A Gentle kiss as his arm wrapped around my waist. The sound of the waves and slight breeze all evaporated as we sank into our own world. Oh man, that was a kiss to remember, a kiss that may never have happened if we hadn't taken out at least a couple of links of ego armor. We both reluctantly broke the kiss, came back in for one more quick follow up and then smiled into each other's eyes. Yep, I thought, I want more of this. He took my hand, we continued our walk, coming back to earth in silence.

Chapter 5

Eilish moves in

Yes, that's right. I figured I may as well fast forward to the inevitable. It didn't take long, about six months. Once we reconnected, it was a mutual feeling of, let's not mess this up, it's too good. We treated it as such and as a result it grew rapidly. Of course, we were aware moving in together could be the catalyst for complete destruction but it's what we both wanted, and we couldn't help it.

As I'm lugging the last box through Brian's front door, there it is—the buttery Florida sunshine spilling across his hardwood floors. My body all jittery and eager, like a kid on the first day of school. This is it. Eilish Thompson, no longer just a visitor in Brian Maclean's world.

"Let me get that?" Brian appears in the hallway. I can't help but think how he looks right at home amidst the chaos of my moving in. Nothing seems to bother him; he is the most even keeled man I have ever met. Actually, I should specify, the most even keeled man when he is around me, but when on the phone for business, that's a different Brian. Kinda sexy to hear his confidence and authority spill out.

"I got it," I say, though my arms are screaming otherwise. But hey, years of restoring houses have given me more than just an eye for crown molding.

As I find a spot for the box, labeled 'Eilish's Miscellany,' I take in the room. It's different already, merging my life into his. Thrilling and terrifying.

"Ready for a break?" he asks, his voice as warm as the coastal breeze.

"Thought you'd never ask." I wipe my brow theatrically, playing up the exhaustion, truth be told, I could go for hours, I am so pumped up. But Brian's boat, a beautiful, 32ft twin engine, Contender, is calling our names, and who am I to deny the siren song of the sea.

The Sea Whisperer, sways gently, tethered to the dock. He helps me aboard with a steadiness that tells its own tale— Brian's unwavering goal is for me to become as skilled at driving this 'tug' as he is. Just in case that day comes when he falls overboard. While I highly doubt that scenario, I have taken to the task with ease and natural ability.

"Where too?" I ask,

"Wherever the mood takes you, captain" he replies, I hear the laughter in his voice.

As the ropes are cast off and I glide out into the calm intracoastal, heading towards the inlet for the ocean, I inquire about the weather conditions for a few hours of fun on the ocean.

Brian says, "It's flat, West 3mph."

"Nice,"

After neatly tucking the ropes away, he is very efficient, he comes up behind me and pulls me close. Both of us look forward, the wind in our faces, smiling. I turn my head to plant a quick kiss and then step out from behind the helm so he can take over. I still haven't quite mastered the inlet, most days it's fine but you never know, and I wasn't in the mood to overdose on adrenaline today, moving in was excitement enough. As Brian navigates, I lean back and watch, this man who seems as much a part of the sea as any creature beneath its surface.

He catches me staring and laughs, a silent conversation that sends a ripple of warmth through me. I love these moments, the unspoken understanding, the shared joy. As we turn towards the inlet, I can feel the strength of the intracoastal and ocean current mixing together, the water beneath us creating a hectic swirl of incoming and outgoing tides fighting for their place in this relatively small, man-made channel. He navigates the bend of the saltwater hallway, avoiding incoming boats while skillfully riding their wake, we finally open out to the beautiful calm, flat ocean, the thrill of making it through and the gift of perfection never gets old. We both yell out "whooohooo!" Brian kicks the boat into full throttle as I stand beside him holding onto the handrails, smiling as big as the vast ocean upon us. This is all I want in life; this is happiness for me. We head to our favorite spot to jump in and snorkel. Brian drops the automatic anchor, turns off the engines. Free of responsibilities, he grabs me from behind and before I know it, I'm in the warm, summer Florida waters, he snatches up our snorkels and jumps in right behind me.

"Don't think you'll be getting away with that Mr." I yell over the loud splash as he hits the water, "There will be consequences, I don't know what yet but watch out, that's all I'm saying."

Brian smiles, he doesn't care, nothing I could do would bother him. Masks and snorkels on, faces down and immediately we are transformed into a different world, a world with life so beautiful, so unimaginably different than land, a hidden secret never seen in person by most. Brian grabs my hand as we weightlessly hover over a deep neighborhood of all kinds of ocean life. He sees something and points it out to me, I can't see it, he keeps pointing and finally let's go of my hand to dive down and give a direct point. Oh wow, yes, I see it, I give a thumbs up, it was a lobster peeking out from under a rock. That's how the next hour is spent. Each of us spotting creatures and sharing this phenomenon with the other. Both of us living our childhood dream exploring ocean nature and not freezing to death in our icy home waters. We must stay close to the boat, even though the anchor has never broken loose there is always a possibility.

This… this right here is why I've packed up my life and plunged in to join his. For the adventure of exploring with another, for the connection— for the pure, unadulterated joy of being with someone who gets you without needing a single word spoken.

We swim back to the boat; I grab the ladder to balance while I remove my fins to climb on board. He is right behind me ready to do the same. I throw my fins up on deck, then climb aboard, Brian's arms on either side of the ladder as I hoist myself up the rungs. I turn to take his fins. That feeling of going from sea to boat always feels like I am on an adventure. I grab towels while he rinses off the masks with fresh water. Wrapped in a warm fresh towel, I head to the bow of the boat to sit and enjoy the heat of the sun, the peaceful breeze. The reality we will both be going back to the same house, not have to worry about did I forget anything in my overnight bag or wonder should I have another glass of wine since I have to drive home, or I should get going since I have to get up early, breakfast together every morning. As all this reality hits me. he comes to join me on the cushions.

He laughs, "What are you so happy about there missy?"

Realizing I was displaying my happy thoughts, I laugh with him, "How could I not be? Look where we are, what we have found in each other, it's all just the coolest."

He squeezes in beside me, "It's pretty cool alright, I get to wake you up in the middle of the night for sexy time, don't forget that little convenience."

I punched him on the arm, "Mr. Romance over here, let's see what happens when you wake me up in the middle of the night."

My head back, watching the clouds float by, out of the corner of my eye I see him nodding his head. He whispered. "Oh, I'm up for that challenge there lassie."

"Are ya now, 4am it is then." I lean over to kiss him.

~

The horizon blushes with the colors and taste of dawn, there's a flutter in my chest that's got nothing to do with the sea breeze. Brian's hand slips into mine, a silent anchor as we stand on the dock, facing what looks like to be our weekend chariot—a gorgeous sailboat, it's sails still furled, patiently awaiting our touch.

"Surprise," He murmurs into my ear with a smile.

"Brian, it's beautiful," I exhale, the words barely doing justice to the swell of happiness rising within me. He rented this for us, a whole weekend getaway on open water, just when I thought my heart couldn't set any deeper into his rhythm.

"Wait 'til you see her dance with the wind," he teases, "She may quite possibly be, actually without a doubt, a better dancer than you." I give him a quick shove dressed in laughter. He has a fair argument.

We're both eagerly buzzing with anticipation to get the walk through from the owner, who obviously has had many a voyage of adventures. I can see the owner's body language and tone relax as he explains all the quirks about his baby, he realizes his boat is in good hands with Brian. Makes me feel proud and weirdly special to see Brian display yet another uncovered skill. The thought of taming the winds, charting our own course with this man of my dreams is exhilarating.

We stow our gear below deck, supplies for two days adrift in our own world. Brian shows me the basics, his hands guiding mine along the lines, teaching me knots that feel like metaphors for something greater—how to hold on, how to let go. Which line to pull for letting the sail out or in, how to connect the wind to the sail. A lot of on-the-job learning, impossible to explain with just words.

As the sun crowns the day with gold, we're out there alone, just us and the vastness of the sea. The sailboat catches the breeze, and we cut through the waves with a freedom that's intoxicating. I take the helm, feeling the pulse of the ocean under my fingertips, the spray kissing my face with salty affection.

"Ready?" Brian asks, as he points at our resting spot for the night.

"Ready!" I yell, my voice almost lost to the wind.

With practiced ease, he takes the helm and puts me in charge of lowering sails, anchoring us in a secluded cove. The world shrinks until it's just the creak of the boat and the sigh of the sea.

"Well done, your first sail lowering expedition, I think that went quite smooth." As he wraps his strong arms around me for a kiss

Brian had some sushi in the cooler and brought the wine I like. I needed at least two bottles of water first; they went down like I was gulping air. We dined like royalty under the sunset of the Florida Keys. It was perfect.

He pulls me close and as the strength of his hold weakens me, our lips meet. With each caress, each whispered affection, the connection deepens —an intimate language spoken in the silence between breaths.

Here, with the hushed lullaby of the ocean cradling us, the city girl who sought solace in the bones of old houses finds sanctuary in the arms of the man who seems to speak the language of the sea.

In the glow of the cabin light, he untied my bikini top letting it fall to the floor, cupping my breasts in his rough hands, my arms fall by my sides as he slides down my body touching me over my bikini bottoms then peeling them off freeing my vagina to the cool air and his warm fingers. I gasp at his touch, my hands rest on his shoulders, he lowers me to the cabin floor as he takes off his swim trunks, revealing his hardness, ready for me. He lowers down to kiss me and takes his cock in his hand to go inside me. He gently, slowly pushes into my wet clit, we both moan in pleasure as he slowly pushed deeper, he backs out, still slowly, to go back in a little harder this time, in and out, until I am ready for him to use his beautiful cock to the full extent of its abilities. As I feel my explosion build, I moan louder and now he is ready too. We both cry out, with only the seagulls to hear, as we join together in ecstasy. our shadows dance upon the walls—two figures entwined in an ancient rhythm as old as time itself. Love, unmoored from everything but the heartbeat of the other, shared moments like these —raw, real, and beautifully ours.

The morning sun winks at me through the porthole, a flirtatious invitation to start the day. I stretch, feeling the gentle sway of the boat as it nudges my consciousness awake. Brian's still asleep, his breathing a soft counterpoint to the ocean's murmur. I watch him for a moment.

"Let's go to Mull," he'd said last night, his voice low and tinged with a vulnerability that made my heart swell. "I want you to meet my mum."

As I slip out of bed, the humid air kisses my skin. What a way to wake up, as I slide out from his hold to sneak outside. I want to take in this stunning place by myself for a moment. Take in the full extent of how fortunate I am, as I remember my past relationships and how far they were from this. I had no idea, and now that I know this feeling of love and fulfillment, there will never be a way to ever accept anything less.

He wants me to meet his mom, the matriarch of the Maclean lineage. Yikes! Okay that thought woke me up a bit more. A ribbon of excitement weaving through the nerves. This is big – meeting the family is big – but somehow, it feels like the natural next step, a new layer to peel back in our unfolding story.

Brian stirs as I kiss him on his lips he kisses me back, still asleep, "wakey, wakey," I whisper. His soft eyes cracking open, all sleepy. "Morning," he murmurs, the corners of his lips curving upwards.

"Morning," I reply, my voice still light with the remnants of dreams. "Ready for a swim?"

"Always," He grins, and there's that flash of excitement, like a spark ready to ignite. We dive off the back of the boat and almost instinctively swim to each other. I push him away with a splash and dive under, feeling the water brush past my fully naked body, he joins me as we make our way to the bottom and then glide up to the surface. Our morning begins as beautifully as the day continued. We breakfasted on deck, cereal with almond milk and banana, breakfast of champions. By the end of the trip, I felt ready to go again, for a week this time, maybe build up to three months, leave it all behind, sail around the Bahamas. One step at a time, first Isle of Mull.

42

Chapter 6

Isle of mull

ian's phone buzzes—a text from the ferry company confirming our ride to Mull.

"Right," he says, pocketing the device, "time to meet Jan." The ferry ride is a transition from one world to another. The mainland of Oban recedes into the horizon, a fading memory, as the rugged silhouette of the island looms closer, it's mostly raw here, unpolished and untamed by human hands, the wind carrying buried ancient secrets.

"Beautiful, isn't it?" Brian's voice breaks through my reverie, his hand finding mine.

"Like something out of a book," I say, squeezing his fingers. The island does feel mythical, shrouded in a mist that makes it easy to believe in magic and lore.

"Wait until you see Tobermory— you will love it." There's pride in his voice, a love for his homeland that resonates deeply with me.

As the ferry cuts through the waves, I lean into the railing, the salt spray just missing my face, tasting the wildness of this place. Brian stands beside me, pointing out landmarks—the jagged cliffs, the hidden coves, and the rolling hills covered in heather. All very familiar to my own roots.

"Jan's cottage is just beyond that ridge," he says, his hand gesturing to a distant rise crowned with green. "Right by the cove."

"Looks beautiful," I reply. The thought of meeting her, of sharing stories and laughs, gaining a glimpse into Brian's past, fills me with warmth.

"Are you nervous?" Brian asks after a moment, his gaze searching my face.

"A bit," I confess, chuckling softly. "Your mum... she's important to you. I want her to like me."

"She will," he assures me, and there's such certainty in his tone that I have to believe him. "You're impossible not to like." I snuggle in closer, he puts his arm around my shoulder and holds me tightly.

Mull grows larger, more detailed with every moment. The ferry's engines hum steadily, a comforting drone beneath the conversations of fellow passengers, all bound for the island.

"Here we go," Brian says as the vessel begins its approach to the dock. He squeezes my hand once more before releasing it to help gather our bags.

Stepping onto the soil of Mull, I take a deep breath, filling my lungs with the crisp, sweet air. This is it—the beginning of a new chapter. I'm ready, ready to embrace whatever comes next. Jan's neighbor and family friend, Edward, is there to meet us and take us to Jan's house. Brian spots him in the carpark leaning on his car smoking a cigarette.

"Whoohoo," Brian waves and shouts his name, "Edward, old man, give us a hand."

Edward drops his cigarette and walks quickly over to greet us.

"Well, well look at you, it hasn't been that long, but I swear you're different every time I see ye. And who is this lovely lady?"

"This is Eilish, the Irish girl I was telling you about. Eilish this is Edward who I completely forgot to mention." Brian laughed.

I laughed, "That is not true Edward, I know all about you and how kind you are to Brian's Mum."

"What, no that must be someone else, Edwin I think." Brian punctuating his joke.

"Come on you idiot," I linked Brian's arm as we walked towards the truck.

I step onto the pebbled path to Jan's house, the sound of the ocean's breath pushing and pulling against the shore filling the silence. In front of us, the cottage with its smoke-filled chimney swirling skyward becomes the backdrop to what feels like a pivotal moment in my life.

"Mother!" Brian calls out as we near the front door, his voice full of delight. The door swings open before he finishes the word, and there stands Jan Maclean, her big smile sends immediate warmth that wraps around me like one of those thick, knitted shawls.

"Brian, my boy!" she exclaims, her arms wrapping him in a fierce embrace. Then her gaze shifts to me, and it's as though she sees straight through to my core—the hopes, the fears, the deep-seated love for her son that I haven't even fully admitted to him yet. "And you must be Eilish. welcome."

Her hug is just as tight, and I can't help but melt into it, surprised by how much this acceptance from a near-stranger means to me.

"Thank you, Mrs. Maclean," I say, feeling a familiarity, I can't explain.

"Please, call me Jan," she insists, leading us inside to where the heart of the home beats with the crackling fire and the kettle singing its welcoming tune.

We settle around the kitchen table, a pot of tea and an assortment of biscuits between us. Jan pours the tea, the steam carrying the earthy aroma seems to weave a spell of ease over the room.

"Brian tells me you're a true spirit of the ocean," Jan says, her eyes twinkling as they meet mine.

"Yes, I have always been drawn to it," I reply, stealing a glance at Brian whose cheeks are tinged with color from the glow and warmth of the fire. We finish up our tea and Brian pipes up.

"Let's show her some of the outside before it gets too late, Mum."

He suggests we take a walk to see his favorite spots. I put on my coat and step outside to the dimming, chilly, fresh evening, giving Jan and Brian a little time to chit chat alone. They both catch up with me, still talking away, as I stroll down the garden path towards the beach. They seem happy and relaxed. Brian comes up behind me, hand on my shoulder, we naturally combine to one. Jan asks about our lives in Florida, and does he miss his ol mother?

"Of course I do, you silly old woman." he jokes.

I never slept so well as I did that night, even better than on the sailboat. The fresh sea air, relaxing after feeling the acceptance of a very important woman, seeing another loose side of Brian, the usual warmth of his body. How could I not sleep soundly. Just as well I did, since what was to come would require a very alert and focused mind.

Brian was already up when I woke up, as I was stretching, he walked in with a steaming hot cup of tea. I reached my arms out towards him, he put the tea down and flopped beside me on the bed, kissing me all over my face.

"Wake up sleepy head," he said as he reached under the blankets to rub my ass.

I screamed, "Your hands are freezing!" As I attempted to squirm away.

"But your ass is oh so toasty warm," he continued to hold me in his embrace. His fingers slipping towards my clit, we start to kiss and as I finally relax and adjust to his ice block hands, he jumps up.

"Okay, up you get, I have all kinds of adventures planned for us today." He states enthusiastically.

I bury my head in the pillow a little let down from his tease. I lean up on my elbow and take a sip of hot tea, The cold, crisp, air sneaks in under the sheets. Best to get this over with, I throw off the blankets, reach for my jeans and sweater. So cold!!

The day started with a big, when I say big, I'm not exaggerating, breakfast. Fresh homemade soda bread, fresh eggs from Jan's chickens, bacon, sausages, fried tomato and lots of tea. I was toasty warm now but needed a minute to digest. This would take a bit getting used to, my usual was a smoothie.

Brian remarked as he was walking out the door, "You take your time there miss lazy pants, I'm going to get the bikes ready from the shed."

I laughed as I chomped on some delicious jam and butter bread, "I'll be right behind you," grinning while leaning back in my chair, cup of tea in hand.

Okay time to pull myself away from the blazing fire and brace the damp Scottish cold. Hat, gloves, layers, a few extra donated by Jan. Hard to imagine the cold when you're packing in 80o heat. As soon as I stepped outside, I was greeted by a sunny, cold, windy day. Brian was at the garden gate ready with our bikes. I was excited now and ran down the pathway to greet the days adventure.

Brian was all business, yet giddy to show me his world. He handed me one of the bikes. It was a heavy old reliable machine that's seen many a salty day and unexpected pothole but surprisingly took to the road with a smooth yet squeaky glide.

"What's our first destination?" I yell over the wind as I follow my handsome, Scottish man. Sometimes I look at him and wonder how did I get so lucky, what does he see in me? I have asked him that and he looks at me in puzzlement.

"Would a list be preferable?" he asks, "Because it's pretty long, or you could accept I see you and love everything about you."

The list seems like I may be pushing my, seemed insecurities, a bit too far so I accept his 'love,' answer. Although secretly, a list would be cool. Who doesn't want a list of how awesome they are?

There is beauty to behold around each and every bend. The landscape is un-surprisingly stunning. It could be as simple as a sheep peeking over his stone wall or a flower growing in the middle of the road, to a wide-open field with rocks haphazardly bulging out of the grass, all so peacefully beautiful. Pedaling up hill on our faithful metal steeds, we turned onto a skinny dirt path, brushing past overgrown blackberry bushes mixed with gorse and thorny hawthorn. I follow in excitement and trust. Brian stopped and got off his bike, I did the same but still didn't know where we were. It felt like the wind picked up but not much else was different up ahead. I thought maybe we were going to pick blackberries. Brian laid my bike on top of his and took my hand, we walked around the corner to a blast of wind and the most spectacular view of beaches, fields, cliffs. Even though I was huffing and puffing up the hill moments before, my breath literally stopped with a gasp, joy written all over my face. He turned and looked at me, I looked back at him and nodded my head. "Yes," I was saying, this is as moving to me as it is to you. He understood my simple gesture and read my face of pure indescribable peace. We had once again added another degree of connection. This was going to be an amazing few days. After sitting in the cold wind and warm sun, wrapped in each other's arms, in and sharing the magnificence before us, we stood up shook and stretched our bodies ready for what's next. We hopped on our bikes and enjoyed the easy downhill ride, out onto the main road.

"Feeling a little hungry?" Brian asked

I had to think for a second, "You know what," I said, "Weirdly, I am!"

"Me too," he said, "follow me."

We cycled for a mile or so, hard to tell time and distance when so perfectly in the moment. It seemed like an imaginary line was drawn and the fields turned to buildings with human action intertwined. Cars and pedestrians, shops, pubs, cafes, restaurants, a little harbor full of boats, sailboats, fishing boats. Good grief, I love this place! We parked our bikes at a restaurant called, The Galleon Bistro on the Brae, it's a little place behind the local post office, right on the harbor. How could life get any better than this I thought, as we sat across from each other in this grounded, solid, warm atmosphere. Everyone seemed so content here, genuine, real. By the time we got through soup, I wanted the waitress to be my best friend. It's just all so easy, without judgement. Even without knowing someone I could feel what a good person and soul they were. I see how Brian has turned out the way he has. We finish up lunch, step outside into the brisk air, Brian now in a t-shirt, me with two less layers but still hanging on to my jacket. As the day continued with discoveries of past hideouts, I didn't want it to end. We finally got back to the cottage and shut the bikes back up in the shed.

Brian said, "There is one more place I want to show you."

We went through a small field, slid down a shallow slope that led to an intimate cove, sheltered by looming cliffs. A little further along the beach was a set of jagged rocks topped with, what looked like, smooth rocks. As we got closer, I could see they were huge seals quietly sleeping, bathing in what little sun was left. When they heard the rustle of sand beneath our feet, I could see the biggest one open his eyes. Within seconds they were all awake barking and clumsily escaping human presence. All but the big one, he stared at us knowingly, almost nodding his head in recognition but still with slight trepidation moving his eyes from me to Brian. He took one last look at me and followed his mates into the waiting safety of the ocean. I turned to Brian in disbelief.

"Holy crap, that was amazing!" I mumbled, "I mean, what the fuck, this Island is beautiful?"

Brian laughed in a proud and confirming way. "I know," He said, "It wasn't easy to leave, I can tell you that."

"So why did you," I asked.

He shrugged his shoulders. "Well as unbelievable as all this is, I knew I had to get out of here and make sure it stayed this way, or at least keep it in the best health possible. That's why I'm in the profession I'm in, I love my job and what it allows me to do but while working on saving this, the sacrifice is to leave it."

I looked at the man in front of me, the man I could not get enough of and now I had another reason why. He is willing to give up everything he loves to save the bigger picture for everyone else, for nature. Most men I dated in the past, were narcissists times a hundred, usually took me a couple of months to see it as they were also master manipulators. I don't think I was aware and as open as I am now. Brian has led me down a path of new doors and they all swing wide open, no hesitation. He makes it so easy for me to walk through and feel safe in the unknown. Every opening has been a door of ease, love and acceptance. In the past the doors were usually stuck halfway or I wanted to go through but couldn't find the key and when I did finally go through, I wondered, why did I want this so much? But the world makes more sense to me now.

We headed back to Jan's cottage only to find a bustling party of locals ready to welcome home one of their own.

"Okay, brace yourself," said Brian.

A chorus of "Brian!" rang out from the small front door where a welcoming crowd of young, old, big, small, beards, functional cloths, pretty dresses, came spilling out to greet us. Beer in one hand and loving embrace with the other. I felt so at home in this sea of strangers. I would catch Brian glancing over at me in the middle of throwing his head back in laughter. Made me feel warm inside, he was checking to see if I was okay. Being on the other side of the room with a party of strangers felt like being in a cocoon of love.

We fell into bed that night, exhausted, full of stories and shared memories. We both curled up into each other's arms and passed out. I woke up around 6am, slightly hung over to find Brian was already up. The house was quiet. I thought that was strange, not to hear him bashing about making breakfast, no sound of him and Jan chatting away. I started to feel unease, I wasn't sure why, there was no reason to think anything was wrong. I pushed back the blankets and got dressed, as I opened the door to our bedroom and walked down the short hallway, I kept waiting to hear movement, but it was quiet.

"What the fuck," I whispered to myself, "This is so weird."

I grabbed my coat and quickly slipped into my boots, they must have gone for a walk, I thought. Since I had no idea where they would have gone and no reason to think Brian was harmed in any way, I mean he grew up here, he knows this place like the back of his hand, I decided I was worrying for nothing and strolled down to the beach. I sat on my bum and slid down the short sandy hill to the cove, I was immediately hit by how different it seemed than last night. The beach felt, smelled different. I could see some seals on the rocks in the distance and there was a couple by the shoreline. I headed further down towards the water, expecting the seals to woosh away, but they didn't. Hmm, then I saw why. There was black stuff all along the beach by the water, the seals were covered in it! Nooo this was horrible, what the fuck happened? I ran at first and then slowed to a walk as I approached the seals, they looked helpless, some of their eyes glued shut with oil, some looked up at me their furry faces screaming fear and pleading at the same time. There was one in particular that came an inch or two towards me, then tried again but couldn't get the strength. it's eyes, bore into me.

"I will be back, I promise, it will be okay, I will be back," I told the seals.

I turned and ran as fast as I could, yelling Brian's name as I approached the cottage. Jan swung open the front door.

"What is it, what's the matter Lass, where is Brian?" Jan asked with alarm.

I looked at her in disbelief, "where is Brian, but he is here isn't he? I thought he was with you," I said in a quivering voice. "He should be back by now. I knew it," I said, "I knew it."

Jan was holding me by my arms trying to calm me down.

"Knew what, Lass, what did you know?"

I barely uttered, "Something is wrong. The seals Jan, I have to get Brian to help the seals."

Jan's face and demeanor changed, "What about the seals?" She demanded.

I just wanted Brian, I got free of Jan's hold and ran back down the path, where the fuck is he, he wouldn't leave this long without telling me. Jan ran past me towards the beach. *But we need Brian*, I thought.

I yelled after her, "Where is he Jan?"

Jan waved me to follow her, perhaps she knew what to do, she didn't seem worried about Brian so maybe I was being an idiot. I followed Jan, getting there in time to see her fall to her knees in front of that one seal who moved towards me. She must know that seal, she reached her hand to touch it, and it closed its eyes, the seal trusted her.

"What can we do?" I asked. I looked around, there were so many of them, not all as bad as this one but still bad. My mind flipping back to, where the fuck is Brian? Getting bagels maybe? Do they have fucking bagels here? Okay I'm losing it.

"Jan I'm going to look for Brian, he must be back by now, he will know what to do." *I mean this is what he does,* I thought, *or rather fights to make sure this doesn't happen.* As I turned to leave, Jan let out a

"NOOO!" filled with pain and sadness.

No? I thought, *why not, he could help, we have to act fast.* I turned to question her, but her face and eyes made me stop and shut up, she waved me down to the sand to sit. *What is going on?* I thought.

"I have to tell you something, something only a handful of people know," Jan said.

My mind racing, *oh okay great, Brian has a wife and kids nobody told me about, of course.*

"Let's just deal with the seals now," I say, "You can tell me later about whatever it is." I noticed the seal staring at me, *I know*, I think to myself, *I want to help you, but this woman wants to talk about bloody gossip.*

"Eilish!" Jan yells.

She made me jump.

"This is Brian!" Jan yelled in exasperation.

Okay, now I think she is crazier than me, she seemed so together. I treated her almost like an upset child, nodding my head in agreement to calm her down, then I can't take it anymore.

"What the fuck are you talking about? Now is not the time to let your crazy out Jan, get up let's go find him and maybe some others to help clean this mess up."

I take off towards the cottage, when I glance back Jan has her hand on the seal, defeated. I feel bad, I didn't handle that in the most caring way. But my gut is being torn apart, I fight the feeling, it's winning. I know something is wrong with Brian, I have to find him.

Chapter 7

finding the oil covered seals

As I cross the field towards the house, I see the neighbor who picked us up at the ferry, farmer Edward. He watches me frantically running across his field of sheep. At first, he had a look of exasperation and slight annoyance while his dog desperately attempts to bring order to the flock after this stupid woman's inability to read the field creates white dots running all over the place. As I get closer, Edward sees something is wrong.

"What is it, Lassie, what's wrong with ye?" He says trying to calm me down. I see him looking around. "Sure, where is Brian, is he not with ye?" The sheep now cornered by his dog, kept in safety from the deranged human. "It's alright now, breath and tell me what is happening."

The old man's touch felt safe, reassuring, made me stop to take the time to explain, I felt like he would know somehow. "It's Brian, I said, the seals…" I was going to go into the whole story of the oil, Brian's disappearance.

He cut me off, grabbed me hard and said, "What about the seals, what's wrong with the seals?"

"They are covered in oil." I said, "But I can't find Brian, he can help!" I try to break loose from his grip, obviously nobody cares about Brian. I need to get to the house, he must be there by now, he is probably looking for me.

"Come with me." Edward demanded.

"What, no, I will meet you down there later!"

"I know where Brian is," he said, "But you have to come with me. Is Jan down there?"

"You know where he is? But I was just down there, and he definitely is not there."

Edward looked at me with a look of command that gave me no choice but to believe him, even though it made zero sense."

"Trust me," he said. He yelled a command at his dog and tore towards the cove as fast as his old limbs would let him. As we slide down the sandy hill, we could see Jan still sitting with the same seal, she had taken off her top to use as a rag in an attempt to rub the oil off.

"Oh Edward! thank GOD, I didn't want to leave him, we have to get him up above to get this off."

"Is it himself?" Edward inquired.

Jan responded by nodding her head and almost whispering, "It is."

Wow these people are really into seals, as devastating as this scene is, why on earth would Edward make me come back here on a false promise?

"What is going on?" I am so frustrated at this point.

Edward kneels by Jan and I hear him say, "we have to tell her Jan, there is no way around it now. I can tell you trust her, and I do too."

Jan nods, as if she's been expecting this moment since we crossed the threshold.

"Tell me what?" I yell making it clear I can hear them, so yes, they will have to tell me now.

Edward puts his hand on Jan's shoulder and then helps her up to standing. Jan takes a couple of steps closer to me, she has her head down, my heart is pumping out of my chest, what the fuck? *This is serious*, I think.

Jan links my arm, "Let's go over here." She guides me to a pile of rocks for us to sit while Edward continues gently rubbing the seal and telling the fading creature it will be okay. I continue to glance up the beach expecting Brian to come bounding down any minute. The wind in our faces, cold air wrapped around our bones, I start to shake with adrenaline and lack of clothing. I realize Jan must be absolutely freezing, I take off my second layer and pop it over her head in attempt for her to capture whatever heat she has left, her hands emerge from the sleeves and reach for mine. Our perished hands hold on tightly to each other, Jan looks into my eyes and starts to talk

"When Brian was a child he couldn't get enough of the sea, he practically set up home by those rocks over there," Jan indicates towards the rocks with her head. Those same rocks were such a beautiful surprise not so long ago and now they were the beginning to a story I felt did not have a happy ending.

Jan continued, "There are a couple of things I have to tell you. Both are not very believable; I trust you will believe. This story is all I have, to explain where our Brian is."

'Our Brian,' those two words made me want to break down, I'm not sure why but it felt like such an honor to share her son's love. The son, that came out of her being, she kept alive, fed and made happy for so many years, creating a bond that nobody could come close to, and I was just given acceptance to be a part of.

Jan goes on, "I have been given a gift."

I sense the gravity in her words before she even explains.

"A gift that belongs to our family, passed down through generations." Jan says with such passion in her eyes.

Jan looks down and I hear her mumble, "Okay here goes." Then with conviction, "I was born a witch." Jan raises her head and waits for my reaction.

"I'm sorry, what?" I ask, pulling my hands from hers and turning away. I'm on a thin line of not wanting to be rude and calling her bat shit crazy, to holding her in my arms until she comes out of whatever zone she is in.

Jan jumps up, "I'm sorry to spring this on you like this and I know you must think I'm crazy, but you have to trust me. The reason Brian is not here is because he was given the gift of becoming one with the sea when he was a child, a gift I gave him."

I look at Jan and yell, "Stop it Jan, you have to snap out of it, we have to find him, something is wrong." Then I say, "Oh God, maybe that's it, he went for an early morning swim and got caught in the oil, we should contact the lifeguards or whatever you people have here, we have to get some boats out there."

Edward walks towards us, he has been watching us.

Jan goes to him, "Is he okay, still with us?"

Edward nods his head, yes. then goes to me. "You have to believe her Eilish, it's true."

I look at them both, one at a time, trying to read their faces. Could it be so? I do believe that witches existed at one time but that was a long, long time ago. Okay so say Jan is a witch, what has this gift got to do with Brian's disappearance? They are both watching me and the seal with a desperate intensity. Then something clicks inside me.

"Oh, shit no, it can't be, there is absolutely no way that is him, no fucking way." My bad language be damned at this point.

Jan and Edward nod their heads and then we all run towards the big lump of defenseless blubber.

"So, you're saying this is Brian, that's what you're saying?" *Come on*, I think to myself, still a far cry from believing all this. "First of all, how do you know this one is him? They all look pretty much the same." After the words leave my mouth and hit the open air, I feel like such an idiot for believing. "This is just a seal!" I yell.

Jan is equally exasperated at this point. "Okay look Eilish, you don't have to believe us but at least help us. Stay with him while myself and Edward get help. We will have to bring him up to the house and that's going to take a few people. We will be back soon, just keep talking to him, stay calm for him Eilish, okay?"

Jan, and Edward take off towards the road, leaving me sitting there with this suffering seal that is also my boyfriend. I laugh a little at the whole ridiculous caper half expecting Brian to jump out of the bushes at any moment. But I know Brian, he would never joke around at a crisis concerning animals. I finally turn my head to look at the seal, feeling a little spooked by the whole thing, but the seal's eyes are so gentle and so tired. Finally, the seal rests his head on my thigh. Holy cow, Brian or not, I have to save this seal, all of the seals. I watch his breathing and, in a panic, for a second, I thought he may have died, but it's okay, there is movement again. I gently continue attempting to remove the oil where Jan left off, but it's futile. There is too much of it and too deep within his coat. Oh, I wish they would hurry up. I sing whatever songs come into my head to comfort him. If it is Brian, he always loved my slightly off-key singing.

"I miss Brian sooo much." tears falling down my cheek. The seal opened his eyes and blinked up at me. It felt like this creature, in obvious pain and discomfort, was attempting to comfort me! That's ridiculous. Okay pull it together this is no time for self-pity we gotta save this seal! As I look up the beach, ready to curse out the rescuers delay, there they were. Must have been twenty locals, a lot of the people from the party last night, all came galloping towards me like wild horses, throwing out clouds of sand behind them. I was told to step back; I gently lift the seals head from my thigh and let everyone do what they needed to do. They had a leather canopy stretcher, like the ones you see in those old war movies. Two wooden poles on either side of the leather. Even with so many people, it was still a challenge to slide this, what was probably at least, 600lb seal onto its rescue bed. But they did it, next was the challenge to get him up to Jan's house, the closest place with warm water. We needed warm water and soap to bathe the oil off. It was going to take all night and probably all the next day to get him free. We had to be careful not to let the oil soak into his skin any more than it had. When we got him to the top of the sandy hill, Edwards truck was ready to take over the load. Someone had pitched a big canopy tent for the upcoming all-nighter of 'operation oil removal.' Once they dropped off this seal it was time to immediately turn around for the next one. I was still not convinced about the whacky story of Brian being a seal but what I believed or didn't believe at this point didn't matter. I was attached to this seal, and I was going to save him. Still hoping Brian would show up and deeply worried about him, I continued to nag Jan about calling someone at the ocean rescue. But all she said was Brian is okay, he is in good hands. Frustrated, I had no choice but to trust her and get on with the job in hand. Everyone worked together and in rotation. I had rubber gloves on but was still covered in oil everywhere else. We had someone ripping up old sheets for rags, it was a chilly night, so the water didn't stay warm for very long, it needed to be rotated every fifteen minutes or so and of course someone was on tea duty. Most of the seals were already taken over to the seal rescue in Oban and when we finish here that's where these guys will join them until the oil is cleaned up from the ocean. As the sun rises and I realize I have been out here all night, picking and wiping away human's poison, tiredness hits me like a dizzying poof of air. I have to keep going, I'm almost finished, Jan is helping me now too. We drink tea and talk softly by the seal, Jan puts her hand on mine and says, "You will have Brian soon, my dear," Jan looks into the seal's eyes and smiles.

Brian has not left my thoughts for a second, I have multiple scenarios of his whereabouts flashing through my mind.

The seal starts to shake, I have heard the oil can remove waterproofing from a seal's fur, making them more susceptible to the cold. Jan quickly puts a blanket over him. All the other seals are gone to the sanctuary, I am so worried about this one. Jan ran back inside to get more blankets, I see the seal looking around, looking at me. I am the only person out here now. The seal gets more frantic and flops about, I scream, "Jan! Jan! get out here something is wrong." She doesn't respond. I have to leave the frantic seal to get Jan, I turn towards the house just as Jan is coming out the front door, her face changes from pure worry and stress to elation, I turn back around, and Brian is standing in front of me. So many emotions came over me, disbelief, joy, relief, anger. He was naked, shaking and fell to the ground. The seal was gone, just it's skin remained.

Chapter 8

Brian's secret

The grass beneath Eilish's feet blurred as she sprinted towards Brian's crumpled form. Her heart pounded, each beat a response to the unbelievable doing a full circle, 'holy shit, it's true'. her head was spinning.

"Brian!" Jan's voice cracked with worry as they reached him.

Eilish dropped to her knees. Brian's skin was pale, his breathing labored.

"We need to get him warm," Eilish said, tinged with urgency and practicality.

Jan nodded, her weathered hands already working to prop Brian up. "The fire. Quick now."

Heavy footsteps approached. Edward's gruff voice cut through the panic. "He's okay!"

"Yes, but the oil," Eilish explained. "He's freezing."

Edward's broad shoulders blocked out the rising sun as he bent down. "Right then. I'll take his legs."

Together, the three of them lifted Brian. His head lolled against Eilish's shoulder. She could feel his shallow breaths against her neck. *Stay with us,* she thought fiercely. *Just hold on.*

They staggered towards the crackling fire, each step an eternity. Eilish's muscles strained under Brian's weight. The smell of peat smoke grew stronger.

"Careful now," Edward warned as they lowered Brian onto the rug near the flames.

Jan bustled around, gathering up blankets.

Eilish met Jan's eyes over Brian's prone form. The older woman's face was lined with worry, but her voice was steady. "He's strong, our Brian. He'll pull through."

Eilish nodded. She cradled Brian's head in her lap, willing warmth into his body. The fire's heat pressed against her cheeks, but inside, she felt cold with fear and shock.

Jan leaned down to Eilish, her arms encircled her, Eilish clinged to the older woman like a lifeline. Tears pricked her eyes as the reality of Brian's transformation crashed over her.

"I'm sorry," Eilish whispered, her voice thick with emotion. "I should have believed you sooner, I thought you had gone nuts."

Jan's gave a quiet laugh as she rubbed soothing circles on Eilish's back. "Hush now, lass. You believe now, and that's what matters. And who says I'm not nuts?"

Eilish pulled back, wiping her eyes, laughing, "It's just... it's all so..I'm just so relieved he is okay Jan."

"He is more than okay, you found yourself an amazing man, ye are a good match?" Jan finished, a knowing glint in her eye.

Brian stirred, drawing their attention. His eyes, usually so vibrant, where clouded with exhaustion. But determination burned beneath.

"The seals," He croaked, struggling to sit up. "I have to see them…"

Eilish gently pressed him back down. "Easy, love. You're still weak."

Brian shook his head stubbornly. "No, the others, are they okay?"

His words hung heavy in the air. Stroking his hair in an attempt to comfort him. "Yes," she said, "They are down at the sanctuary, everybody is helping, you need to rest for a bit, they will be okay."

Brian's body relaxed and he fell back asleep

Eilish's hand found Brian's, squeezing tightly. Remembering images of the devastation she saw that night. The shock of it all surfacing. Full of thoughts of frustration, anger, sadness towards the havoc the oil spill had created. Something had to be done, with the technology they have today there is no excuse for this to happen. It wasn't just the seals but otters, birds, fish will all be suffering. She took a deep breath and brought her focus back to what was in front of her. Her reason to feel alive was dying before her eyes.

"We have to do something," Eilish said, determination hardening her voice.

Eilish looked up at Jan. "What do we do now?" Eilish asked softly.

Jan's gaze turned towards the sea, her expression unreadable. "Now, my dear, we fight."

Brian's breath hitched, a painful rasp cutting through the room. His hand flew to his chest, face contorting.

"Brian?" Eilish's voice sharpened with alarm.

Jan leaned in, gently probing Brian's abdomen. He winced, a low groan escaping.

"The oil," Jan muttered, her brow furrowed. "It's got to him more than we thought."

Eilish was adamant. "That's it, we need to get him to a hospital."

"Aye," Jan agreed, already moving. "Edward! We need your help, let's get those clothes on him!"

Brian's eyes fluttered open, unfocused. "No... I'm fine..."

"You're not," Eilish said firmly, cupping his face. "We're getting you checked out, no arguments."

As Edward rushed in, Brian grabbed Eilish's wrist. "Wait," He rasped. "The others...?"

Eilish hesitated, her chest tight. "I don't know, love. But we'll find out, I promise."

Brian nodded weakly, his voice barely a whisper. "They're scared. Confused. I need to help them."

"First, we help you," Eilish insisted, fighting back tears. "Then we'll save them all, okay?"

Brian's eyes met hers, his old determination shining through.

As they prepared to move him, Eilish thought, about how much she loved him and would do anything for him. She felt love for him before, but this love felt like he was physically a part of her now. His pain was hers.

~

The tires screeched as Edward took a sharp turn, his knuckles white on the steering wheel. Brian slumped against Eilish in the backseat, his breathing labored.

"We're making a detour," Brian announced, his voice tight.

Eilish's head snapped up. "What? But Brian you need.."

"The sanctuary," Brian wheezed, suddenly alert. "We have to check."

Jan had called ahead to make sure the ferry at Craignure was still at the dock. When they pulled up to the boat, it was waiting for them. As soon as the car was on board, the boat was underway. Everyone on the island knew what happened the night before and a few knew the important role Brian played in all of it. The ferry was at full throttle to get to Oban.

The car lurched to a stop outside a weathered building. Salt air mixed with antiseptic hit their senses as they stumbled through the doors.

Inside, chaos reigned. Volunteers scurried about, arms full of towels and medications. In makeshift pools, semi-oil-slicked seals barked weakly as the volunteers took them out one by one to clean and heal.

Brian pushed away from Eilish, stumbling towards the nearest pool. His legs gave out, and he crawled the last few feet.

"No," he choked out, reaching a trembling hand towards a motionless form. "Oh god, no."

Eilish's heart shattered as she realized—two adult seals and a tiny pup lay still, beyond help.

A volunteer approached; her face drawn. "We lost them an hour ago. The others... we're doing what we can."

Brian's shoulders shook with silent sobs. Eilish knelt beside him, wrapping her arms around his quaking frame.

"I'm so sorry," she whispered.

He turned to her; eyes red-rimmed but determined. "Help me up."

"Brian, you need.."

"Please."

She couldn't refuse him. Supporting his weight, they moved to the edge of the largest pool. The remaining seals stirred; their dark eyes fixed on Brian.

"Listen," he said, his voice rough but steady. "I know you're scared. I know it hurts. But you're safe now."

The seals inched closer, drawn by his words.

"Soon, the ocean will be clean again. You'll swim free, I promise." Brian's voice cracked. "For now, let these people help you. Rest, heal, don't give up."

A low, mournful sound rose from the seals. Brian answered with a noise deep in his throat—a sound Eilish had never heard a human make.

She held him tighter as he swayed, spent by the effort.

"Hospital," she murmured. "Now."

Brian nodded, his eyes never leaving the pool. "We'll be back," he promised the seals. "You're not alone."

Edward said he was going to stay at the sanctuary to help and he would give regular updates to Brian. This seemed to bring a small piece of relief to Brian's load.

Eilish's fingers gripped the steering wheel now as she navigated the winding coastal road to the hospital, Jan yelling directions. Eilish's face in full alertness, swerving around cars, glancing back at Brian in the back seat with Jan. "How is he doing, is he okay?"

"Yes, lass, just keep your eyes in front of you, don't kill us all for God's sake. You're almost there, next right and you should see the signs." Jan said.

"Oh, yes there it is, there it is." Eilish yelled. "I'm going to pull up in front."

She pulled up at the front of the hospital, cutting off an ambulance, Eilish jumped out and zipped around to open the back car door helping Jan with Brian. The ambulance crew, not too happy initially, but then saw Brian's condition and grabbed a stretcher. Turns out their patient had a broken foot, so Brian became priority. Eilish and Jan were told to step back while the doctors and nurses did their job. The hospital workers quickly got a respirator and iv in Brian, then assessed what to do next. I realized it was best for Jan to explain Brian's condition and what had happened to him since she knew how to spin the story and not give away his secret. Finally, they got Brian in a stable condition which allowed us to go back and see him. He was so pale and drawn looking, but his eyes were alive and happy to see us walk through the door. I couldn't get to him fast enough, to touch him, hold him, although it proved to be a little tricky bending and winding around all the IV's. The nurse came in and told us not to panic it all looks a lot worse than it is, he will be fine, may even be out by tomorrow. Jan was on one side and me on the other, all three of us relieved and happy for our own reasons.

Jan got up and said, "Do you know what, I'm parched, I could murder a tea or coffee, even the watery stuff they have here would be nice, will I get you anything?"

"No, thanks," Brian and I said in unison. I was alone with my love, I wasn't sure where to start, I didn't want to upset him or get him worked up so I didn't ask, he will spill when the time is right.

Brian broke the momentary silence, he squeezed my hand and simply said, "I know it's a lot and I will explain, I promise, but for now I want to enjoy being safe and alive here with you."

I nodded my head in understanding and smiled, leaned in to kiss him. I smacked my lips, "Hmmm what is that taste, can't quite place it?" We both laughed.

"Okay smarty pants, I haven't brushed my teeth in a while and raw fish has a way of sticking around. I can't wait to be home with you." We both smiled. Just then Jan walked into the room chattering about how nice a nurse was and how she couldn't get the coffee machine to work.

"What are you two grinning about, may I ask?" she asked.

We said, "Nothing." Both of us aware Jan knew very well why we were smiling.

I didn't want to leave but the last ferry was going soon, and Brian needed his sleep. We met the nurse on duty that night and I had full faith he was in good hands. I had brought him his phone so there was that too. Brian insisted we stop in and check on the seals on our way home.

The drive home was a completely different experience, I could actually take in my surroundings, unlike the frantic, hellish drive here, full of uncertainties. It was starting to get dark, and we didn't have much time, but we did stop at the sanctuary as instructed. Edward had just left with one of the other volunteers, we will probably see him on the ferry. Everything was under control the seals seemed calmer and they were resting. No more deaths and it didn't seem like there would be any more, they got through the worst. I turned to Jan and said, "This can't happen again, surely? It just can't."

"In a perfect world, lass, but we will continue to do what we can, there are a lot of obstacles to climb, mainly people and corporations. I thought this Brexit business would help with improving the Marine Protected Areas but who knows. Anyway, we can talk about that more tomorrow. I don't know about you, but my brain is exhausted. Thank God these seals are coming through okay. We better get a move on to the ferry, up bright and early in the morning. If I know my Brian, he will walk out of that hospital and swim home if we don't get there first thing."

~

It was so nice to finally have Brian sitting here beside me in the comfort of Jan's cozy space. He was looking and feeling so much better today, still not himself but close. Of course, we made a stop at the sanctuary and after a couple of hours he had to be dragged away to have his forced, Dr prescribed rest. The seals perked up when they saw him, they too doing much better. Amazing to see the undeniable connection between them, understandable now that I know his secret. I felt the volunteers had an inkling too but it's such an outrageous idea or concept, nobody would say a word at the risk of sounding, bat shit crazy. As we sipped on our cups of hot tea back at Jan's, relaxing by the fire, I felt it was the right time for me to raise the obvious and much needed questions, I couldn't hold it in anymore, so out it came.

"Talk to me guys, I need the full story, I mean what the...?" I turned to Brian, "You're a seal, an actual seal, how, why? I know about you being a witch Jan and you gave the power to Brian, but I feel there are a lot of details missing, like what have you been doing as a seal, are you a seal in Florida too, does anyone else know?" I could have kept going but by the looks on their faces I knew they got the idea, I needed answers.

Brian put his hand up to Jan and said, "I got this Mum," He turned to me and held out his hand for mine.

"Very few people know, Edward knows and a couple more of mum's friends and now you, of course. There have been only a handful of people the spell works on, so I am honored to be blessed with the gift of 'The Change,' that's what we call it but the official term is Transmogrification. Anyone granted 'The Change' can use it only for good. If I ever tried to use for greed or bad I would get transformed back to a man in the middle of the ocean and most likely drown."

Jan interjected, "No fear of that with my Brian, no, he doesn't have an ounce of badness in him, never did. He was even a cooperative toddler." Jan lovingly smiled at the memory.

I smiled too at the thought of this brave, handsome, grown man once being a cute little 3yr or 4yr old boy. Brian now feeling the wrong attention, cut us off from memory lane.

"Okay, okay, so anyway," he swept his hand in the air at the sentimentality as if to whoosh it all away, he continued with his exclamation, "No I have not been a seal in Florida and was not originally planning on staying there for long, but I found it to be a great base for what I was working on. Battling for universal change in how we treat our oceans, basically. America being the most powerful country in the world, I decided to set up camp there and see what I could do. Also being a seal in Florida may have brought a little unneeded attention. There are a lot of reasons no one can know. One being, I don't want to be a lab rat. Trust me if I was discovered I'm pretty sure you would never see me again. Brian put his head in his hands at the thought, "What I have, cannot ever be discovered." Brian emphasized, "I felt I could trust you very quickly after we met, and I still feel very strongly that you are in my life for many reasons."

I felt it too. I thought. The day we first met, sitting across from each other having coffee, felt right. I have always thought that. Even with our momentary separation and my surface doubts, I knew there was something there worth fighting for, waiting for. It sounded like a cliche when I heard my couple friends describe how their relationships started or when they proclaim it in romance movies, 'it felt right.' Well, I am here to announce to myself and the world, "it felt right." Validating to know I was not wrong in this magical feeling. Brian and I were in a flow of togetherness.

Chapter 9

Investigation

The once-tranquil bay was a hive of activity. Boats crisscrossed the water, unfurling massive orange booms. On shore, figures in hazmat suits scurried like ants, their movements urgent and precise.

"Christ," Eilish muttered to herself, watching from the front door as the scene unfolded. The enormity of it all hit her like a physical blow.

"How's Brian?" Jan asked as Eilish stepped back inside.

"Still sleeping, stable, but..." Eilish trailed off, gesturing at the chaos before them. "What's all this, then?"

Jan's sleepy eyes narrowed against the rising sun. "The beginning, I'm afraid. Come on inside, I've put the kettle on."

"Jan," Eilish began, cradling the warm mug, "What aren't you telling me?"

The older woman sighed, sinking into her chair. "I've seen spills before, but this... the speed of the response, it's not normal."

Eilish leaned forward. "What are you saying?"

"I'm saying," Jan's voice lowered, "That either someone other than me knew this was coming, or..." She paused, her gaze distant. "Or something else is going on."

"Okay explain, I mean surely they've stopped the leak, what else could it be?" Eilish asked.

Jan's eyes met hers. "That's what we need to find out, lass."

Eilish sat for a minute with her tea, pondering the situation, then turned to Jan, "Wait, what do you mean, 'someone other than me?' You knew this was going to happen? How could you know, why didn't you stop it if you knew? What was Brian doing out there if he knew about how dangerous it was? He almost died Jan!"

"Hey, hey slow down relax, come on, put your coat on let's go for a walk, I don't want to wake him up." Jan put her tea down and walked towards the coats.

Go for a walk? I didn't want to walk I wanted this woman to talk. She is right, there was something going on here, bigger than what I already knew and something more she wasn't telling me. Seriously, I thought I had my fill of un-relatable surprises and now I felt another one coming on. "Fine," I muttered, stomping over to grab my coat. Jan watching with a half-smile at my childish reaction.

Jan quietly closed the door behind us, and as we braced the crisp morning air, I realized I was being a little demanding. "Sorry to be so up front Jan but please no more secrets, this is all so hard. I will crack up! I am barely digesting the seal thing as it is."

"Aye, I know lassie, it's okay, come on let's go this way." Jan led me towards a hilly field that ended on a cliff with a magnificent view over the ocean. The land of never-ending views, it really was amazing. Jan indicated we should sit, she started to talk.

"So, as I mentioned, I am a witch." Jan said towards the sea then turned to me to make sure I was listening. I nodded, she continued. "Part of being a witch is having premonitions. Brian came home a few months ago, because I saw this disaster happening. Sometimes my visions are crystal clear but not this time. This time I saw the oil a boat and where it would happen, but not when. We got to work finding the routes of any major tanker vessels. Brian did his best every day to warn the creatures. Realizing my vision was not materializing, we concluded it wouldn't happen for a while and more than likely I would get another vision closer to the spill. So, he went back to Florida." Jan went on," Now, when I got really sick a few weeks ago, fever etc., I did have a vision, but again fuzzy, you see. Brian had just been here, and I know the importance of his work in Florida. I didn't want to waste any more of his time with another one of my vague visions. Well, turns out, it wasn't a fever dream and now all I can think about are those poor seals and all the other animals that will be affected. All this probably from a simple missed mechanical issue." Jan explained. "Something rusted out because a person missed it or didn't bother to check. So anyway, Brian went out that morning to make sure everything was still okay, yes, well it wasn't. I told him not to go, my vision was weak, but my gut was strong. He just said, 'don't worry, it will be fine.' he wanted to go for a swim, and he would be back for breakfast." Jan shook her head in regret. "Thank God, you found him, and he is okay." She put her hand on my arm and smiled. Then changed as a worrying thought brought her back to our living stresses. "I have to find out what's going on with me and why my powers weakened, and we have to make sure that blasted trawler company pays for all this."

I sat there, listening, absorbing, understanding. Going back to when Brian got that phone call on our first date. This must have been the emergency, no wonder he rushed home. Damn I felt so guilty for thinking all those bad things about him. There was no way he could have explained this and I'm sure he didn't want to lie. It's all coming together now, well kinda, this was a lot. So, Jan can see into the future and can make a person 'Change' into a seal!! How crazy is that? Jan put her hand on my back and asked.

"How are you doing lass? I'm happy to see we haven't scared you away on the ferry already," Jan laughed.

I gave her a gentle but firm shove on the shoulder and then joined her in laughing at this whole wild scenario.

"Right let's get back before himself wakes up and decides to go for that swim." We both laughed again, knowing it was only a matter of time before our worn-out joke came to fruition.

As we approached the cottage, we could see through the window's net curtains, Brian's shadow moving across the wall.

"Here we go," Jan Said.

When we opened the front door, the floorboards creaked under Brian's bare feet as he paced the living room, phone in one hand, steaming cup of tea in the other. He almost looked like his old self.

"Yes, I understand that, but it really doesn't explain the details of the collision. I think it would be better if we meet in person, would it work for you if I came by your office tomorrow? Okay great see you then."

Eilish watched him from the corner of her eye, relief and concern battling within her.

"Well, you look and sound a lot better." I said as I went for my greeting hug. Felt so good to have his strength wrapped around me once again, giving confirmation of his healing.

"I cannae just sit here," Brian growled.

"Well, you can't chance going back out to the ocean either, not as a seal anyway, you could take the boat though." Jan said as she reached into the fridge for sausages. "What's the meeting tomorrow?"

"Yes, would you come with me Mum? This is an important one, it's with Marine Scotland. I have an appointment with the director. Something is not right here. This mess was made by an oil tanker coming to close to shore and they are trying to say it was the fishing boat's fault, an accident. It doesn't make sense." Brian turned to Jan at the stove. "Right? You said in your vision it was the tanker that collided with the fishing boat, didn't you?"

Jan stopped what she was doing and turned to him, "Brian as sure as I am standing here it was the tanker going into the fishing boat, it was a fuzzy vision I will give you that but there is absolutely no doubt who was crashing into whom."

Eilish went to Brian placing a steadying hand on his arm. "Brian, you've only just recovered. Are you sure-?"

Brian turned to Eilish with a look of understanding and patience, he took her face in his hands and kissed her, "I know this has been a wild ride and along with everything that has been put in front of you, you are worried about me, and I love you for that. But time is not on our side, this has to be figured out." They hugged and Eilish was able to relax just a tiny bit after Brian's comforting words.

Brian and Jan looked at each other, Brian nodded to Jan

"Eilish have a seat for a minute," Jan instructed "One of my other gifts is reading minds, it is a very delicate spell and one I don't use often or lightly. If we are wrong and this director is a good person and not up to anything underhanded, well that's not good for me. You are supposed to use it only when you are pretty certain you are dealing with an evil entity. We have been following her actions and seen who she deals with, and even though we don't have much to go on, I know she is hiding something"

"Okay, I give up on being shocked or surprised anymore, there is obviously a lot more to come." Eilish was talking more to herself than any listening ears. "I accept all and let all things enter without a fight." She threw her hands up and smiled at both of them.

Brian laughed, "That's my girl." We all laughed and sat silently for a minute.

"So, what now?" Eilish asked.

Jan jumped in, "Now we eat." It was more of a command than a suggestion. "Brian grab some eggs from the chickens, would you?"

We all ate enough for an army; we hadn't really eaten in two days.

Brian asked, "Where is the skin, Mum?"

Jan didn't look up from washing the breakfast dishes, "It's in the bathroom closet, still need to get the rest of the oil off. I can work on that if you two want to take the boat out. You were lucky to be able to transform back in the condition it was in." Jan turns to Eilish, "Usually if the skin is not in the right condition, it won't change or change back if it's damaged as a seal."

"I know," says Brain looking at Eilish. "Watching you worry, not knowing what was going on. Well, it gave me that extra kick to change back and thankfully it worked."

Jan smiled, "Ahhh the power of love, nothing stronger. Okay so the keys to the boat are in the usual drawer. She is still moored down at the harbor; someone will give you a lift out."

Eilish and Brian cycled their bikes up to the harbor shed and sure enough Brian's old friend Brodie was there cleaning up his boat.

"No way, is that you Brian? Sure, how long has it been? I heard you were around last month or so, but I must have missed ye, well you're looking… well a bit pale for a Florida native." Brodie went on, "Oh now, who is this lovely Lassie?"

I smiled at Brodie's charming way, Brian, squeezed my hand as he introduced me.

"This is Eilish, my girlfriend, you're going to be seeing a lot of her Brodie, hey listen would you mind giving us a lift out to the boat?"

"Not at all, not at all, jump in, your mammy had me start her up every couple of weeks or so, just to keep her oiled and charged, you know."

"Brilliant, thanks, that's perfect. Seemed to be running well when I was here last. So, what's going on Brodie any gossip I should know about?"

"Ahh sure not a thing worth repeating, just the same old stuff. A few more frustrated fishermen for sure but that's about it."

As they pull up to Brian's boat, Brodie leans in and says something to Brian, I couldn't hear over the sound of the engine. Brian nods and has a look of worry.

"Okay there now Eilish," Brodie yells, "Grab that line there behind ye, the one on yer fella's boat." Brodie winks at Brian.

"Okay Brodie, thank you, you can go now," Brian says in friendly annoyance.

Brodie laughs as he pulls away, he makes the phone sign up to his ear and yells, "Ring me when ye get back, I'll meet ye at the pub."

Brian gave a quick wave and nod to Brodie while getting the boat ready. He slowly pulled out of the harbor weaving around the moored boats, The seas are a lot rougher here, but this boat was built for Scottish turbulant waters. It wasn't an open design like the boat we had in Florida this one had a small pilothouse with big windows protecting you from the wind and rain. The boat itself was about 23 feet, the perfect size in my opinion. *What an amazing experience I was having,* I thought, but then reality hit. *Okay so here we go, time to see what is going on out here.*

Brian explained, "Some people on this Island do not want me here, a lot of the locals work on the oil rigs, and they feel I am a threat to their livelihood. I get that and they are right, I am, but I am working to find a way to keep everyone happy. Tons of oil can't continue to spill, it simply can't go on, it's a threat to everyone. The fishing trawlers are another big hazard not only to the ocean but also the local fishing boats. The small local boats go out and come back empty, that's happening more and more these days."

I listen to Brian's frustration over the roar of the engine and realize more what he has ahead of him. We slowed down about a mile from shore. The sea was calm now, he turned off the engine and we just sat on the bow of the boat in each other's arms. He wanted a minute to relax before we got to the site. The spill happened about two more miles north of here. He wanted to see for himself the Port of Registration on the side of the fishing boat.

Brian said, "Look for a series of letters and numbers on the side of the boat. That will tell us who owned it and if it was stolen." He turned to me with a smile, "Alright, now let's get going. I just needed that quick snuggle before we head off."

We saw the boat in the distance before we got any closer, we stopped to look through binoculars, seemed like it was all clear. The half-sunk boat had those red booms floating around it to keep any further oil from spreading.

Brian pointed, "There it is, the letters we need, here take the wheel and bring us in a little closer." As he balanced on the bow, He took pictures with the binoculars built in camera.

"Hmmm," he was thinking, "Yep, Brodie was on the money It's one of the local boats all right, but I wasn't expecting so much oil, okay let's get out of here."

I reversed and brought her about heading south for home.

We pulled up to one of the docks, he said it would be fine there for a couple of days, usually they don't let you tie up overnight, but we will be fine.

"let's go to the pub," Brian said as we walked arm in arm up the dock.

"Okay I said," A little surprised that was the direction we were going after the weird discovery of an abundance of mystery oil.

"The pub," Brian said, "is a den of information."

Ahhh now it made sense. We walked along the harbor to a pub called Mishnish and sure enough there was Brodie with a few other locals. Brian waved.

Brodie waved us over and greeted us both with a friendly smile.

"Well, well, sure it is good to see you taking time to relax and have a few," Brodie said and then addressed me, "You don't see him in here often, Lassie. You bring out the playful side of himself. What will ye have?"

Brian and Brodie went back and forth about who was going to buy the first round, Brian won.

"Listen Brodie, will you come over here and sit down for a minute, I want to talk to you about something?"

Brodie looked at Brian to read his face, apparently these two have known each other since they were born.

"Come on so, let's grab that table over there before it's gone." Brodie said, he led the way to a quiet end of the pub.

We sat in the corner with our pints Brodie, and I looked at Brian waiting to hear what he was going to say.

"Right so, Brian," Brodie said knowingly, "Out with it, I know you found something, 'not right' out there."

"The crash happened way too close to shore, Brodie, what was the tanker doing so close and you're right it is Callum's boat. Callum would never let this happen. How did they come to the conclusion it was his fault?"

Brodie nodded his head, "They said he was drinking,"

Brian through back his head in frustration, "What! We both know that's not true." Brian was shaking his head, 'I know.'

"You know how it is, it's us little guys against the giants." Brodie said feeling defeated.

Brian asked, "Is he okay?"

Brodie looked at him, "What do you think?"

"So have you talked to him, what did he say?" Brian asked.

Brodie nodded his head, "I have, here is the thing Brian," Brodie paused and looked at Brian and then at Eilish.

"You can trust her, I promise, "Brian said, "Tell me, what really happened?"

As I listen in to the conversation, I could only catch half of it over the hum of people talking but I could see their faces and it wasn't just Brian worried now.

Chapter 10

Meeting with Mabel Gage

rian was more determined than ever to get to the bottom of it all. But he wanted to make his first stop this morning at the seal sanctuary. Brian and Jan go over their plan of how to indirectly get into Mabel Gage's mind, yet directly enough for her mind to be read. As they go to leave, a knot formed in Eilish's stomach. "I'm coming." Eilish announced.

Brian tells Jan to go on ahead to the truck, he pulls Eilish into him in a tight hug, then leans down to gently kiss her warm soft lips, "Eilish don't be an idiot, you have to stay and watch the fire, make sure it doesn't go out." Brian smirks.

"I have to stay and watch the fire?" Eilish says in a both humored and threatening voice. "Do I now, for what, so I can have a nice cup of tea for you when you get back, is that it?"

"Well, that would be nice, but they have electricity for the tea now. Ahh Eilish come on, I don't want to put you in any unnecessary danger." Brian pleads.

Eilish nods her head, "Okay go on, I love you. But just so you know, Brian Maclean, sometimes I like being in danger and I decide when I put myself in that danger." Eilish looks into Brian's eyes then kisses him.

Brian understands who he is dealing with, he quickly holds her hand and gives one last squeeze before taking off towards the waiting truck, "I love you too."

Eilish smiles at the doorway, nodding her head.

Brian and Jan stop by the sanctuary first. Brian has been checking on the seals with the volunteers and aquatic vets via phone. He was told they were doing well and would be released within the week. He was finally fit enough to see them in person before they go back home to the sea. As Brian opened the doors to the rough, cold damp building, he could hear the commotion of healthy, lively, excited seals. They were being loaded into crates to be released.

"Oh Brian, I'm so glad you're here," said one of the volunteers, "They seem to calm down when you show up."

Brian smiled, "Happy to help," he approached the stack of crates with stressed out seals. As soon as he got close, the heavy breathing stopped, and the commotion of panic came to calmness.

The volunteer, piped up, "See what I mean," he said to anyone that would listen. "They are getting released earlier than we had projected, so that's good news all around. They are healthy enough and looks like they did a great job cleaning up the ocean."

Brian breathed into each crate and the individual seals snorted back. He was telling them it was okay, and he would see them soon. They appeared to 100% understand. To anyone around it was a deep heartening experience, including Jan. It made her proud. The seals got loaded onto a truck and were taken down to their now cleaned up beaches. Brian's spirits where alive and awake. Now he was really ready to fix this. Enough was enough.

Brian and Jan pull up to the Scottish Marine office in Edwards truck. The government building loomed, all glass and steel.

"Okay," Jan said, "How do we explain me being here? It's a bit unusual to have your mother tag along, don't you think?"

"It will be fine," Brian dismissing Jan's worry, "I'll think of something."

The two exit the elevator to Mrs. Gage's floor, her front desk ready to greet them as soon as they turn the corner.

"Brian Maclean to see Mabel Gage, I have a 2:30pm appointment."

"Yes of course, Mr. Maclean, and you are?" The receptionist asked Jan.

"This is my mother Jan, I can't get rid of her," Brian says with a friendly laugh, "I'm just home for a few days and Mum wants to see a bit of what I do, would Mrs. Gage mind?"

Jan looks at Brian with a half-smile topped off with a 'I will kill you later,' look.

"He is my only son, I can't seem to let go," Jan says in a confidential whisper to the receptionist. "Do you have children?"

"Aye, I do yes, a wee girl," the receptionist takes out a picture of her daughter."

"Oh, what a love," Jan says, "You must miss her when you're here."

The receptionist smiles and nods her head while putting the picture away. She picks up the office phone and announces, "Your 2:30pm is here Mrs. Gage."

"Send him in, thank you." says the voice through the speaker.

"It's the office straight at the end, Mrs. Gage is expecting you." The secretary indicates for Jan to go too.

"Brian, so nice to see you again," said Mabel Gage a young, friendly woman sitting behind a desk with a computer, a pile of papers, a phone and a few pictures from her recent wedding. "And this must be your mother, I can see the resemblance."

Jan says, "Forgive my intrusion, I came into town with Brian to pick up a few things and decided I may as well get a glimpse of the man in action. Just a proud mother, I won't be a bother." Jan found a chair to the side and sat quietly.

"Not at all Mrs. Mclean, anytime."

Jan smiled.

"So, Mr. Maclean what can I do for you? You sounded upset on the phone."

"Yes, it's about the oil spill, I appreciate the speed in which it was cleaned up but I'm just trying to figure out what exactly happened and see if I can contribute my services in any way to a preventative plan you have already set up, or plan on setting up. maybe we could work together?"

"Oh, that is very kind of you Brian, I really appreciate that. Yes, it is a horrible scene, I got the clean-up crew in as fast as possible and of course we are doing everything we can to help the animals affected."

"Yes, that's great, I saw that. I was wondering if you had a chance to actually see the leak site and did you think anything unusual about it." Brian watched closely as Mrs. Gage answered.

"I haven't had a chance to get out there, but I have seen pictures from the cleanup crew and some drone footage, nasty stuff, nothing unusual though, no."

"Would you mind if I had a look at those pictures?" Brian asked.

Brian glanced over at Jan as Mabel rooted around on her desk. Jan's eyes locked onto the woman, her expression inscrutable. Brian knew that look. She was reaching out, probing, trying to slip past Mabel's mental barriers.

"Of course, here we go," She proudly produced the requested evidence.

He looked at the pictures and nodded, "Okay, I see, yes, I have seen worse, Has the captain told you what happened? How did the leak come about and what happened to create the spill?"

"Yes, yes Captain Callum, unfortunately had a few too many drinks, engine got caught up in his fishing gear, then of course he couldn't get out of the tanker's way on time, and they collided. Oil and gas just leaked out all over the place, really stupid incident. I will of course, make sure Callum is fined heavily and his license will be taken away for a year."

"Well, that is just crazy, crazy stuff," Brian turns to his Mum, "Did you hear that, nuts right Mum? A few too many drinks can create such devastation, terrible. And may I ask, was the boat found inshore, within the 12 mile or did this all happen out a bit, further offshore?"

Mrs. Gage's polite smile never wavered, but her knuckles whitened as she gripped her pen.

"Good question, I'm sorry I'm not certain on that but I can email you as soon as I get more information." Mrs. Gage was ready for Brian to leave now she felt like she was going down a dark hole somehow. The tension in the room was palpable, a silent battle waged beneath the surface of polite conversation.

"Yes, an email would be great, thank you." Brian turned to his mother to gesture to leave then turned back to Mrs. Gage. "Just one more thing, didn't you send the crews out to do the clean up, you must have had the coordinates, no?"

"I didn't personally send them, no that is another department," said Mrs. Gage getting flustered but mostly keeping her cool.

"I see," said Brian, "You weren't interested to see where it happened, if it was within the 12-mile line?"

"I'm having a meeting this afternoon to get updated on the details, I have a lot going on Mr. Maclean and I realize this is an important issue but there are other important issues that have priority. I hope you enjoy the rest of your stay; you have been lucky with the weather."

Jan jumps in and shakes Mrs. Gage's hand, "Let's not take any more of the busy woman's time Brian, I have to get those sheets before the shops close, don't work too hard now, take care."

"Yes of course," Brian shakes her hand, "Thanks again for your time. I am here for a few days so if there is anything I can do, please don't hesitate. I love this place, and I would do anything to help stop these spills from happening."

"Thank you, Mr. Mclean, I appreciate that, I know you have made a lot of progress with similar issues in the States."

"Yes, accidents will keep happening but most of the time they are unnecessary incidents that can be prevented. Okay, listen, I will let you get to the rest of your day, take care."

Brian and Jan wave at the receptionist as they exit towards the elevator. Jan leans on Brian in the elevator, she is drained. Jan's grip tightened on Brian's arm as they exited the building, the cool sea breezes, a stark contrast to the stifling tension they'd left behind. Jan senses Brian's worry, "I'm fine, I'm fine, I just need to get to the car." Brian guides Jan to a bench by the front of the building, then goes to fetch the car.

He runs around to help Jan then safely buckles her in.

Right before Jan fell asleep, Brian commented on his mother's choice of an excuse, "Sheets, really that's what you came up with, sheets?" he jokingly remarked.

"I actually do need sheets, all you bloody seals destroyed mine," said Jan followed by a deep snore.

Eilish is waiting for them when they get home, she sees Brian helping Jan out of the truck. Worried, Eilish runs down to meet them.

"Oh my God, what happened, is she okay?"

"Yes," Brian says, "It's all part of the process, she will be fine just needs a few hours' sleep."

Brian and Eilish get Jan into bed then head out to the Kitchen. Eilish is bursting to know what happened and what is this 'process,' Brian is talking about. Jan looked like she was drunk.

"I'll put the kettle on," Eilish says grabbing the kettle and filling with water.

"Perfect," Brian says as he slumps into a chair.

"Are you too pooped to talk about it?" Eilish leans over the back of Brian's chair and whispers in his ear, "What about an outline?"

Brian Laughs, "Okay sit," Eilish eager to know what happened, obediently sits.

"I think we got something, babe. For sure something is not right. I asked pretty basic questions, and she either couldn't answer or wouldn't. The distance from the inshore line where the spill occurred is a crucial detail. You and I know it was approximately eight miles out, but she seemed hesitant to confirm. And her pictures of the oil spill showed a different spill than what we saw in person. The oil in her photos was much less than what we saw. It's possible more leaked out between when she took the pictures and when we arrived, or the pictures were photoshopped maybe? I don't know but it's something."

Nighttime hit and Jan was still sleeping, "I'm just going to check on her before we go to bed," Brian said as he quietly stepped towards Jan's room.

"Okay, well I'm going to have a quick shower," Eilish said grabbing Brian for a kiss.

"Don't use all the hot water, I will be right there."

Her eyes were closed while the shampoo ran down her face, she heard the shower curtain being pulled back and then a cold hand on her waist as he kissed her neck, his other hand sliding down her body, cupping her small, smooth and soapy, firm breasts. Squeezing her nipple and gently caressing and squeezing her ass, she let out a light groan and pushed her hips closer to his. The soap washed away from her eyes; she could see the water cascading down his perfect body. As she tasted his warm tongue, her hand ran down his wide strong back, they kissed deeply. His other hand now moving from her ass to her throbbing clit. Gently touching, rubbing with only the warm water between them, she reached down to feel his cock, his hard cock, she put it between her legs. Both wrapped up in each other and themselves. He leaned around her to turn off the water then reached for a towel to dry them off. He takes her by the hand to the bed where she lays down and he climbs on top of her, slowly pushing inside, leaning down to kiss her passionately while he continues to fill her body, the pressure of his hips pushing his hard cock so deep it hurts in the most exciting way pain can feel. Out and in until they are close, then he pushes harder and faster both of them trying to be quiet, but she let out a squeal of ecstasy. He can't hold back, and his quiet groan of release comes seconds after. He stays inside for a moment enjoying the connection, then gently slides out and flops alongside her. Their usually lively conversation was silenced by sheer exhaustion, and they drifted into a peaceful slumber, wrapped in each other's warmth.

Chapter 11

Jan's vision about Mabel

Brian and Eilish woke up to the sound of the kettle whistling, a shrill cry piercing the morning silence of Jan's kitchen. Eilish nudged Brian as she whispered, "Brian, she's up, your mum is up." Brian turned his sleepy head to Eilish's face for a morning kiss. Then he quickly pushed the covers off, "Oh shit, she's up, come on get up," he said.

"I'm up, I'm up," Eilish said laughing.

Brian put on his t-shirt and jeans as he quickly walked to the kitchen, cold tile on his bare feet. "Mum you're okay," he said with relief, "I mean are you okay? You seem okay."

"Brian would you ever sit down, you were always too much for me first thing in the morning," Jan proclaimed.

"Sure of course I'm okay lad, just had to process it all. I don't know what's going on with me and my…" Jan turned to greet Eilish, "Good morning, lass, well you two look nice and rested,"

Brian cut her off, "Mum, please what happened?"

Jan goes to sit with her tea, "Right yes, so what was I saying, right, I was wondering why my powers are not as strong, but anyway so here is what I got from miss snooty Mabel. There is money connected somehow, I saw a foreign oil tanker, French I believe."

Brian mumbles out loud to the room, "So it is true."

Jan asks, "What is true, the hush money Callum took? Yes, unfortunately that's true. Who told you that, Brodie?" Brian nods his head. "But it's more than that, much more. How many crew does Callum usually go out with?"

"I don't know, he usually goes out by himself, but he has taken up to two or three, why?"

Jan is thinking out loud, "Hmmmm well there were a lot more than that on his boat in my reading, I can tell ye that. I don't know what's going on, but he is up to no good. A sad state of affairs. I will have to have a talk with that young man."

Brian looks to Jan, "So you couldn't see who they were or why they were on his boat?"

Jan shook her head, "No."

"I think I will go and meet up with the seals, maybe they can tell us more."

Jan nods her head in agreement, "That's definitely the best place to start. We don't want to be going around asking questions and spreading rumors, that could be dangerous."

"I tried to read her mind," Jan continued, voice barely above a whisper. "But it's... clouded. Like trying to peer through thick fog."

Eilish putting it together. "So, you think Mabel's involved?"

Jan nodded grimly. "I do. But we have to be able to prove it."

The kitchen fell silent, except for the distant crash of waves against the cliffs. Eilish met Brian's gaze, they both knew they had a long way to go to resolve all this and there were dangers involved.

Jan's eyes flickered between them, a mix of pride and fear. "Be careful," she warned. "There's more at stake here than we know."

"Right, time to go and have a chat with the seals," Brian said, "They'll know what's happening out there."

Eilish couldn't hold back her excitement. She'd seen Brian transform back to a man before, but not to a seal. The idea was still very hard to wrap her head around, but it did send a thrill through her. "You're going to change?"

He nodded, already moving towards the door. "It's our best shot at uncovering the truth." Brian stopped and turned to Eilish, "Are you coming?"

As Eilish got up from the table, Jan intervened.

"Brian, she can't go, how can she go? I have tried keeping up with you on the boat and I know that boat and the water, she would just get lost out there."

As Brian and Jan were discussing Eilish's decisions on life like she wasn't there, Eilish was already dressed and halfway out the door.

Once Brian noticed Eilish was already gone he put his hand up to his mother to end the discussion.

"It will be fine Mum." Brian said in a, 'finished the conversation,' tone. He went out the door and called to Eilish.

"Look Jan is right you would never be able to keep up on the boat and I don't want the drones to spot anyone out there digging around." Brian is thinking, then asks, "Would you want to come to the beach with me? I'm not sure how long I will be out there but if you get bored you can always come back here."

Eilish starts heading over to the bikes, "let's go!"

"It's about a mile away." Brian said while she leaned in for a kiss.

~

"Ready?" Brian asked, his voice low.

Eilish nodded, unable to speak. Still in awe of this miraculous ability to go from human form to the animal world. Brian had already put on his 'Seal-Skin' he took a deep breath, then dove from the beach into the crashing waves. The transformation was instant – sleek fur, streamlined body, flippers where hands had been. A seal's head broke the surface, intelligent seal eyes meeting Eilish's gaze.

"Holy crap, be careful," Eilish whispered. Then she yelled over the crash of the waves, "Brian is that you, do you understand me, can you hear me?" *Shit we should have come up with signals or something*, Eilish thought. The seal came close enough to flap its tail and splash Eilish with freezing cold salty water. Eilish screamed, "Brian!" She laughed, "Okay I suppose that is clearly Brian, no special signals needed." she mumbled.

Brian let out a soft bark, then disappeared beneath the waves. Eilish stood still by the water's edge, straining not to lose him in the dark, impenetrable, grey water. He was even cute as a seal, Eilish laughed to herself, maybe cuter.

Minutes ticked by, Eilish's imagination ran wild. What if he couldn't find his way back? What if something attacked him?

A splash nearby made her jump. Brian's seal form surfaced, he dove again, this time staying visible. Eilish watched, mesmerized, as he swam away.

In the distance, dark shapes moved. More seals. As Brian approached them, his movements were suddenly different – more deliberate, as if speaking. The other seals circled him, their bodies twisting and turning in what seemed like animated conversation. Brian was now lost in the mix, as much as Eilish tried to spot him out of the herd of seals, it was impossible.

Eilish held her breath, wishing desperately she could be there with him. What were they telling him? Did they know about Callum's boat, about the tanker, their connection?

Silence stretched, broken only by the waves hitting against the shore. A couple of hours went by, Eilish thought about going back to the house and wait for Brian there, but she couldn't get herself to leave. She sat on the beach, thinking. Sifting sand through her fingers, listening for splashes, picking her head up every few seconds to see if she could see him. It was the longest couple of hours of her life. Then, a familiar head broke the surface. Brian swam towards her.

Brian hauled his sleek seal body onto the beach. In moments, he shimmered and transformed back into his human form, gasping for air.

"Eilish," he panted, his Scottish brogue thicker than usual. "It's pretty much what we thought."

The seal skin fell to the sand, Eilish handed him a towel, her fingers trembling. "What did they tell you?"

Brian's eyes were haunted. "The tanker... crashed into Callum's boat alright."

Eilish's breath caught. "But why would they.."

"When they hit Callum's boat the oil started to leak out, it wasn't a big leak. The tanker's dive crew got to it pretty quickly, so it could have been a lot worse. It was still enough for the tanker to have been delayed fined and possibly then have to retire the ship, if they got caught. A very expensive mishap. The tanker shouldn't have been that close to land. The seals said another boat like Callum's showed up and helped with the leak. Then the tanker took off and the other fishing boat left."

A chill ran down Eilish's spine. Yes, it was close to what they had predicted but getting it affirmed, somehow made it feel infinitely more dangerous.

"We need to tell Jan," Eilish said, her voice barely audible. "And Brodie. They need to know what we're dealing with."

Brian nodded. "Aye, but we have to be careful. If someone's willing to go to the extent they did to keep this quiet, who knows what else they might do to keep their secrets?"

Eilish met his gaze, seeing her own mix of fear and resolve reflected. "What have we gotten ourselves into, Brian?"

He took her hand. "I don't know, love. But we're in it now. Brian called Jan and Brodie to tell them to meet him and Eilish at the pub."

~

The pub's warmth enveloped them as they entered. Brodie was already seated in a secluded corner, his face etched with concern.

Eilish slid into the booth. Brian's knee pressed against hers, a silent reassurance, then Jan showed up two minutes later, she sat on the other side of Brian.

"Well?" Jan leaned forward, her eyes sharp.

Brian's voice was low, urgent. "It's close to what we thought but the tanker used Callum's boat for a coverup and there is another local boat involved."

Brodie's weathered face paled. "Christ almighty," he muttered. "Another boat? Callum didn't say anything about another boat."

Jan silent, still, listening, then said, "Money."

"You really think so Jan?" said Brodie. "We have known wee Callum for yonks and you know as well as we do that he loves nothing more than to go out on that boat, it just doesn't fit that he would give it up for a bit of cash?"

Brian nodded his head in agreement, "That's what we have to find out, why would he do this, him of all people?"

As the buzz of the pub started to build with newcomers, the four bewildered crew sat in the corner in deep thought and bursts of chatter.

"First, we have to find Callum, see where his head is at. If we can get him to talk, then we will know a lot more of what's going on." Brian said

Brodie said, "I know he was struggling with the fishing. Since Brexit everyone's quota of catch has been cut down drastically. Thank God I'm a mechanic and don't have to rely on catch. It's been hard on the fishermen though."

"What do you mean 'quota'? I thought Brexit was going to be positive for fishermen?" Eilish asked

Jan jumped in, "I did too, but I stay out in my cottage I don't hear much of what's going on."

"It's been a mess for fishermen," Brian said. "Locals were given a bigger quota, meaning they could legally catch more fish per boat, but the quota given was for the wrong kind of fish, fish no one wants, and the big trawlers are out there hauling in the popular fish, like the cod. And on top of all that the seals and otters need a lot of fish to survive, I mean, the fishermen used to shoot the seals regularly. So basically, fishermen are going through it at the moment."

Jan says. "You think the fishing is so bad that Callum is having a hard time surviving? His family always seemed to have a comfortable life from fishing."

"We all know Callum and his attachment to that boat of his," Brodie said, "It's his baby, his escape, he loves the water as much as you do Brian."

Brian nodded his head in agreement, "I can't believe the fishing has really gone so bad that he would sacrifice his boat and his living for a payoff, must be some payoff."

It was all starting to press down on Eilish. She'd come to Scotland for love, not to play Nancy Drew and figure out possible mass fraud. Yet here she was, caught in a web that seemed to tighten with each passing moment.

Brian held her hand under the table. "Aye, and we need to watch each other's backs. This isn't just about saving the seals anymore."

Eilish looked at each face in turn – Jan's quiet determination, Brodie's gruff concern, Brian's fierce protectiveness. Whatever it is, they would figure it out.

The pub door creaked open, and Mabel walked in, her cheeks flushed. You could tell by the sway of her walk, she had had a few already. She made it to the bar having snippets of chat along the way with her constituents. People were surprised to see her in here, It's not exactly a great campaign strategy. Someone bought her a shot and to our surprise, down the hatch it went.

Mabel swayed on her stool, giggling at something the bartender said. Her usual prim demeanor had crumbled, replaced by loose-limbed ease.

Jan's eyes flickered. "This is good, now's our chance," she whispered. Jan got up and walked over to the happy politician. "So how are you there Mrs. Gage, good to see you again, are you well?" Jan knew as soon as Mrs. Mabel Gage saw her face she would be reminded about their earlier meeting and her mind would start taking off.

Jan didn't want the scene to look weird to any onlookers, so she behaved like she was having a normal conversation all while getting Mabel into a trance. Jan waved her hand at the group to come over so they could surround Mabel in case she collapsed. The spell broke, Mabel had no idea what had just happened, she blinked, confused, then shook her head as if to clear the haze, she hopped down off the barstool and ran to the bathroom to be sick.

Eilish looked at Jan, "Did you just do what I think you did, and I know you know what I think so…?" The group lightly laughed.

Jan said, "I did, and it was much clearer this time, she was too guarded before."

"I've got what I wanted," she whispered, voice trembling. "Let's go sit back down."

Eilish leaned in. "What did you see?"

"Fragments... but enough." Jan's eyes were haunted. "Mabel, she's involved. Deeply."

Brian tensed up a bit. "How?"

"Two local boats. They... they were helping hide people, not the oil." Jan's words came in a rush. "Mabel orchestrated it all. Payments from the tanker, hush money."

"So, let's start with talking to Callum," Brian said.

"Oh, and another thing," Jan said, "Mabel's new husband is also involved. I saw Mabel and her husband fighting and her husband kept giving her the phone, telling her to call someone."

They exchanged loaded glances, the weight of their discovery settling on their shoulders.

Jan straightened, her eyes flashing with renewed purpose. "I'm not as sleepy this time," she said to herself. "We've got work to do then."

Brodie leaned forward, lowering his voice. "I'll have a chat with the local fishing lads, they might know something."

Eilish felt a thrill of purpose mixed with quite a bit of fear. Her gaze swept over their determined faces, a lump forming in her throat.

They raised their glasses in a silent toast, the clink of glass on glass sealing their unspoken pact to figure out what trouble Callum was in and put an end to Mable's corruption.

Chapter 12

Talking to Callum

The pulsing beat of the music reverberated through Eilish's chest as she surveyed the crowded pub. Laughter and animated conversations melted into a festive, warmth.

Eilish leaned close to Brian's ear. "Quite the turnout?"

Brian nodded. "Aye, everyone's keen to let loose. It's been a brutal season." His eyes scanned the room and suddenly fixed on a point in the distance. "Okay there he is, and he is on his own, Brodie, will you stay here with Eilish? I won't be long."

"Oh, now Brian, you sure you want to leave me alone with your lovely lady?" Said Brodie with a smile.

"Ha, I'm not worried, this one is well able to put you in your place," said Brian, as he leaned in to kiss Eilish before heading over to Callum.

Eilish looked over to see Callum nursing a pint, his broad shoulders hunched. Poor lad. Losing his boat had been a terrible blow. Even though he took a payoff, she still couldn't help but feel for him.

"Come on then," Brodie said, nudging Eilish. "I'll grab us a couple of drinks."

Making their way to the bar, Brodie signaled for two pints. As they waited, snippets of conversations around them played out - talk of quotas and markets, of empty nets and strained budgets. A definite thread of unease wove its way through the merriment.

Eilish glanced over in Brian's direction and saw them shake hands, Brian clapping the other man on the shoulder. He leaned in, saying something that made Callum smile. She trusted Brian knew what he was doing and didn't tread too hard. Callum was a vital part of all this, and we needed him to open up.

The barman slid the drinks over, Brodie thanked him, pressing bills into his palm. Eilish took a fortifying sip, relishing the refreshing crispness of her pint of Harp.

Brian's brow furrowed as he studied Callum's face. "You alright, mate? You look like ye've seen a ghost."

Callum shifted, his gaze darting away. "Aye, just...just a lot on me mind, you know? With the boat an' all."

"I can only imagine." Brian's voice softened with sympathy. "Have you thought about what you might do next?"

A mirthless laugh escaped Callum. "Wish I knew. Not many options for a fisherman without a boat."

"Ye've got skills, Callum. Ye'll find somethin." Brian paused, his head tilting. "Speaking of your boat....people are saying you didn't see the tanker before it hit you, is that it?"

Callum's shoulders tensed, his jaw clenching. "You know how people talk, Brian. Always makin' a mountain out of a molehill."

"Aye, that's true enough." Brian's tone remained casual, but his eyes sharpened. "Still, it's a bit peculiar, isn't it? Those tankers are giants, and loud Ye'd think ye'd see it coming, and you drinking? Not like you Callum."

"Yeah, I know, I'm going through stuff at the house, you know yourself." Callum brushed the blame aside. "By God that was a fair bit of oil alright, enough to get a big bloody fine and my license taken away. But sure, what do I care now about the license, no boat anyway and no work to be had on anyone else's boat." Callum's words came out clipped, defensive. "My boat's at the bottom of the sea now Brian. Whatever folks are sayin, it doesn't matter anymore." Callum's posture remained rigid; his expression guarded. "And, you know how things get exaggerated. Best not to put too much stock in rumors."

"Fair enough." his tone lightening. "Listen, if there's anythin' I can do to help ye, just say the word. Ye've got friends here, Callum, don't forget that."

A flicker of something - guilt, perhaps - passed over Callum's face. "I appreciate that, Brian. Truly. I'll sort it out. You don't need to worry about me."

Brian nodded, but the concern didn't leave his eyes. He, of course, knew there was more to the story, but he also knew if he pushed too hard it would only make the man retreat further.

"Listen do you want to go outside for a minute, too much going on in here I could do with a bit of air?" Brian asked Callum.

Callum looked at Brian's face as if to question his realness, was this the same Brian he grew up with and could trust? Callum nodded, "Sure we may as well, I could do with a smoke anyway."

Brian and Callum stepped outside onto the balcony, the cold night air a welcome respite from the stuffy heat of the pub. The muffled laughter and chatter faded as the door swung shut behind them.

Callum gripped the railing. He stared out into the darkness. Brian leaned against the wall, giving him space but staying close.

Callum balanced his pint on a small table and took out his cigarettes, offering one to Brian, Brian shook his head no. Callum lights up, the glow from the lighter revealing lines on his face from worry and a fisherman's life. "It's all gone to shite, Brian." Callum's voice was rough, barely above a whisper. "The boat, my livelihood... I don't know what I'm going to do."

Brian's heart clenched as he watched Callum's defense come down. He'd never seen his friend so defeated. "Ye'll figure it out, Callum. You always do."

Callum barked out a harsh laugh. "I know, I always do but not this time. I'm in too deep. I've made a right mess of things."

"What do you mean?" Brian kept his tone carefully neutral, even as his mind raced.

Callum shook his head, still not meeting Brian's eyes. "I can't... I shouldn't say. It's better if ye don't know."

Brian pushed off the wall, moving towards Callum. "Whatever it is, you can tell me. I'm here for you, mate. Always have been."

Callum's shoulders slumped, the fight draining out of him. "I took the money, Brian…from the tanker. They paid me to keep quiet about the oil."

The confession hung heavy in the air between them. Brian closed his eyes briefly, a mix of disappointment and understanding washing over him. "Why, Callum? Why'd you do that?"

"I had no choice." Callum's voice cracked. "I wasn't going to get insurance money for the boat, stopped paying that a long time ago. The bills piling up because the fishing is so bad... I had to think of my family. I couldn't let them suffer anymore. My wife and kids had to go to her mother's house, I wasn't making enough to keep us all going, you know how much that kills me, Brian?"

Brian sighed, the weight of the situation settling on his own shoulders. "I get it, mate. I do. But this isn't the way. Ye've got to come clean, make it right."

Callum finally turned to face him, eyes glistening with unshed tears. "And then what? Face the consequences? Lose whatever I have left?"

"Ye'll lose more if you don't." Brian held his gaze, unflinching. "Yer integrity, yer self-respect... those are worth more than any payoff."

"Brian, I have already lost that," said Callum looking away, conflict etched into every line of his face. Brian could practically see the war raging within him – a desperate need to protect his family battling against his own moral code.

"I can't Brian, I would go to jail, everyone around here would hate me, not to mention my in laws. It wasn't my fault. The bloody tanker rammed right into me, that captain was the idiot, he was the one that was drinking and fell asleep or something. And now for a bit of money they want me to say it was me, I was the drunk one, I was 'drunk,' Imagine, me drinking out on the boat? I wouldn't do that in a million years, you know that."

Brian did know that. Callum's dad was a drinker, and Callum always swore he would never drink while out fishing and as far as Brian knew, he never did.

Callum went on, "Look it happened and I was paid to keep quiet about it." Callum leaned into Brian, "I'll tell you what is more likely to happen is if I come forward and say I got a payoff, of course those bastards will just deny it! I want to get them too, I love this place, all these big corporations are swallowing us up."

Brian is listening and thinking, Callum is right, why should he take a risk of going to jail when the tanker captain was being reckless. There has to be another way.

"Okay Callum let's see if there is another way, I will start digging tomorrow. No promises but someone has to pay for this," Brian paused, looked over at Callum, "And I would rather it wasn't you."

Callum drew in a shaky breath, "You're a good friend, Brian. Better than I deserve, but you know what's done is done."

"None of that, now," said Brian

Callum let out a heavy sigh, it felt good to share his burden. Now he had to trust Brian was going to keep it to himself or at least not drag him down with any final outcome of justice.

And for now, that was enough.

Brian and Callum lingered on the porch for a bit longer, a silent promise of support. The distant laughter and chatter from the pub seemed to fade away, leaving only the weight of their shared history and the challenges that lay ahead.

"Remember when we first started fishing together?" Brian asked, a wistful smile creeping across his face. "We were just a couple of wee lads, barely tall enough to see over the gunwales."

Callum chuckled softly, the memory temporarily pushing aside his worries. "Aye, I remember. Yer da' would get so frustrated with us, always underfoot and asking a million questions."

"But he never turned us away." Brian's smile widened. "He knew how much we loved it, being out there on the water. Feeling like we were part of something bigger than ourselves."

Callum nodded, his gaze distant. "It's in our blood, isn't it? The sea. The fishing. It's who we are."

"Aye, it is." Brian sighed, his expression softening.

"But it's getting harder every year Brian," Callum solemnly said. "The big drifters coming in, overfishing the waters. The illegal boats causing trouble. And now, with Brexit..." He shook his head. "It's a right mess." Callum's shoulders sagged under the weight of it all. "I don't know how much longer we can keep going like this. The paperwork, the regulations, the packing companies charging an arm and a leg... It's bleeding us dry."

"And crew?" Brian asked.

"Mostly immigrants now." Callum's tone was heavy. "Cheaper labor, and they don't complain about staying on the boat for weeks at a time. But it's tough on them too. No one's winning in this situation."

Brian leaned against the wall; his gaze fixed on the distant horizon. "We've got to do something, Callum. We can't just sit back and watch everything we love destroyed."

Callum's eyes narrowed. "What can we do? I will help anyway I can Brian, but I can't go to jail. You have experience with this kind of thing going up against corporations and governments. I'm glad you will be able to stick around to dig a wee bit more."

"We start small." Brian turned to face him, you're right you can't turn yourself in, you shouldn't, it's not right, what you did, but it's worse what they did and we have to find a way to stop not only the tankers and their bloody leaks but the big trawlers too. If it keeps going like this, before we know it, there will be no small fishing boats, then no town."

Brian deep in thought, took a breath and said, "I'm going to go and find my girlfriend and head home, I will talk to you tomorrow. You are alright then Callum, don't talk to anyone else okay," Brian gave Callum a quick hug. "Right okay then, take care."

Callum nodded to Brian and watched him leave as the door slowly closing behind him. He felt a smidge lighter in his chest. It was a daunting prospect, taking on forces so much bigger than themselves. But with Brian on his side, it felt possible.

The morning sun streaked through the curtains, casting a warm glow across Eilish's face. She stirred, blinking away the last fog of sleep. Beside her, Brian's steady breathing filled the room, a comforting rhythm.

Eilish slipped out of bed, padding softly to the window. She drew back the curtain, gazing out at the sparkling expanse of green fields followed by the ocean. The sight never failed to take her breath away.

"You're up early." Brian's sleepy voice drew her from her thoughts. He propped himself up on one elbow, his hair adorably tousled.

Eilish turned, a soft smile playing on her lips. "Couldn't sleep, too much on my mind."

Brian's brow furrowed. "From last night?"

Eilish nodded, moving to sit on the edge of the bed. "I mean, where do we start?"

Brian sat up fully, his expression serious. "I know. We start with proof, we need proof. We can't just accuse them without evidence."

"Yes, true." Eilish's voice was distant, thinking. "We could start digging, maybe go back out to the site and see if we missed anything?"

They sat in silence for a moment, the enormity of the task ahead settling over them. They were up against powerful forces. It wouldn't be easy.

Eilish stood then tugged Brian to his feet. "Come on. We've got work to do."

Camera

The boat lurched forward, cutting through the waves with purpose. Spray misted Eilish's face as they picked up speed, she gripped the Cockpit side handrail.

"You alright there, lass?" Callum called over the wind's howl.

Eilish beamed back. "Never better!"

The coastline became a blur as they sped towards the crash site. Eilish couldn't help but be in the moment and feel joy from both the wind in her face and the slapping of water against the boat's hull, pure freedom. She glanced at Brian, who had a focused expression on his face as he skillfully guided the vessel.

"How much farther?" Eilish shouted over the noise of the engine.

"Ten minutes, tops!" Brian yelled back.

Eilish embraced the motion of the boat, bending her knees on every impact, she had found her rhythm.

Brian pointed to the right, "Dolphins," he yelled. "Hey Callum, can you take over?"

Callum nodded and smiled; he knew what was coming. He gave Brian a friendly dig on the upper arm as he slid in behind him to take command of the wheel. Callum slowed down giving Brian the balance he needed. He loved to see Brian 'change.'

Eilish was confused. "Wait, are we here?" She asked looking around, "I don't see a thing?"

Brian and Callum laughed, "Not quite yet, my love," Brian said, as he reached into the console and dragged out his seal skin.

Eilish laughed as she saw what was happening, "Awesome!"

Brian came over and gave her a kiss before the final zip up. "I may have a little snack while I'm down there, so I want to make sure I get my kiss in now." he laughed.

"That's it, from now on, we bring a toothbrush and toothpaste wherever we go." Eilish's laugh was silenced by Brian's lips as he held her close. Eilish felt a momentary relief of the Scottish wind while wrapped in his warmth. She didn't want it to stop. Brian released his grip and went to the back of the boat, with one last zip of his suit, he was diving into the water as a seal.

Callum and Eilish watched him surface and then vanish, leaving a slight ripple behind. In moments the boat was surrounded by dolphins and seals, it was spectacular. Brian was lost amongst them, but they knew he was near. Callum carefully navigated the boat back towards the planned destination, making sure not to hit any of our friends.

Eilish turned to Callum, "You knew?"

"Yes," Callum said, "I am one of the few that know, we used to come out here when we were kids and do what we called 'cheat fishing,' Brian would find the fish and I would drive the boat, of course by the time I got there the fish were well gone but it was a fun game. I don't know if Brian mentioned that my da was a drinker," Eilish shook her head 'no.' Callum continued, "well Brian's mum used to take me in all the time when he would go on a bender. My mum died when I was little in a car crash on the mainland. Fishing has been my life."

Eilish looked at Callum with a new light, it explained the closeness that emanated from the two friends.

The boat slowed as they approached the crash site, the engine's roar fading to a low purr. Eilish's anticipation peaked, her eyes scanning the horizon.

"Here we are." Eilish said.

Callum nodded grimly. "Aye, this is the spot."

The water stretched out before them, deceptively calm. Couple of pieces of debris within the circle of booms holding little of what was left of the oil in place, a black and rainbow-like sheen on the surface.

Callum leaned over the side, squinting. "Looks like they've done a right job of cleaning up. Now where is that Brian?"

No sooner had the words come out of Callum's mouth when Brian splashed in front of him, getting him soaked.

Callum laughed, "You get me every time! get up here we have work to do."

With Callum's help Brian scooted on to the swim platform and changed back to his naked form.

Eilish was on the other side of the boat looking at another seal thinking it was Brian until she heard Callum yell out.

"Eilish, over here, bring a towel with ye."

Eilish turned around, "But I thought you were over here…"

Brian stood on the platform grinning and shivering.

Eilish suddenly jumped into action to grab a towel.

Brian quickly wrapped himself in the towel doing little jumps in an attempt to warm up. He climbed over the transom and opened up the towel to capture Eilish for body heat, she screamed and jumped away.

Brian still grinning said, "What's wrong, I only had a couple of fish, come give me a hug."

Eilish was hiding behind Callum screaming, "Brian!!! Don't you dare, my love has slime and fish breath limits."

Callum turning away, "Ey it's just as scary to me, put that towel around ye before I throw you back in."

Brian laughed and went to use the handheld, freshwater boat shower to rinse off his 'sealness' and quickly got dressed.

Callum asked, "Any more info from your buddies?"

Brian looked at Callum for a second and said, "No, nothing new."

Eilish snuck up behind Brian and wrapped her arms around him, whispering, "You and your 'change' will always be the most amazing and the most horrifying thing that has entered my life." She laughed

Eilish then went on to say, "I do feel a twinge of embarrassment for professing my love to another seal. But it's all good; hopefully he'll be able to move on."

Brian laughed, "Heartbreaker. I'm sure I'll hear about it next time I see them."

Eilish inhaled sharply, immediately regretting it as a wave of nausea hit her. The air was heavy with an acrid, chemical smell that burned her nostrils and made her eyes water.

"Christ," She coughed, "That reeks."

Brian explained. "Aye, that'll be the dispersants. Nasty stuff."

He glanced longingly at the water, a flicker of frustration crossing his face. "I could get a better look if I could just..."

"No," Eilish cut him off firmly. "It's too dangerous. I know they cleaned most of it up but still. We already know what that cocktail of chemicals can do to you."

Callum nodded in agreement. "She's right, mate. We need to find another way."

"Wait a minute," he exclaimed, "Didn't you install that camera last month, Callum?"

Callum's expression was a little apprehensive. "Aye, I did! But..." he thought for a second, "I have one on the bow and stern. No way to get it off unfortunately, not in this. We'd need to wait a week or so."

Eilish bit her lip, thinking, then turned to Callum. "Wait, what kind of camera?"

Callum casually said, "just one of those night vision cameras, can't remember what its official name is, everyone has them now."

Eilish still thinking and checking something on her phone then announces, "That's what I thought!"

Both Brian and Callum at the same time, "Thought what?"

"Those cameras usually have an app that stores all the footage," she said.

Callum stood in silence just staring at Eilish. Brian and Eilish where not sure if Callum was happy about this revelation and then he snapped out of it.

Callum's eyes suddenly widened, his hand flying to his pocket. "Hold on a wee minute, you're right!" He blurted out, "I'm a right eejit! The footage... it's all on my phone!"

He tapped the screen frantically, mumbling under his breath. "C'mon, ye bugger..."

Eilish watched Callum's face intently, searching for any sign of success or disappointment.

Brian edged closer, his usual quiet demeanor giving way to barely contained impatience. "Well? Is it there?"

Callum's thumb hovered over the screen. "Aye, it's here. But..." he swallowed hard, 'I dinnae know what we'll see."

Callum pressed play. The three huddled around the small screen, the boat gently rocking beneath their feet, as they waited for the truth to unfold before their eyes.

The grainy footage flickered to life, choppy waves filling the screen. Callum's hand shook slightly as he held the phone, his eyes wide and unblinking.

"There!" Brian shouted, jabbing a finger at the display. "Hard to tell, what's going on here Callum."

Eilish leaned in closer, catching her breath. "Oh my God," she whispered.

The image wobbled, then steadied. A massive tanker loomed into view, its hull gleaming in the moonlight. The camera lurched violently, then went dark.

"Christ almighty," Callum muttered, his face pale, "I didnae realize how close and big it was."

Eilish in shock. "They could have killed you, Callum."

Callum nodded grimly; his jaw clenched. "Aye," he looked up, "Shame about the camera cutting off, we almost had them."

Brian shook his head. "Callum's right, this is not enough, we didn't see direct impact and it's not clear who was to fault, but it's something."

Callum pocketed his phone, in shock and frustration.

Callum sat on the boat's gunwale, "We should talk to Brodie, see if he's got anything more."

"Yes, let's head back, nothing here." Brian said, spinning the wheel. The boat lurched, cutting a sharp arc through the choppy waters.

Eilish gripped the railing. She glanced at Brian, "What if they find out we are working on this?"

"They won't find out," Brian said looking at both me and Callum.

The coastline grew larger, Tobermory's colorful buildings coming into view. As they neared the harbor, she spotted a familiar figure on the dock.

"Perfect, there's Brodie," Brian called out, while easing the boat towards the pier.

Brodie waved, his beard ruffling in the breeze. "Oi! How'd it go then?"

Brian killed the engine, tossing Brodie a line. "We've got something you need to see, mate."

As they disembarked, Eilish couldn't shake the feeling they were being watched. She scanned the docks, her nerves on edge.

Callum's face had a look of defeat, he couldn't hold it in, his voice dropped to a harsh whisper. "I have one more bit of info, so It was Angus MacLeod's boat was the other boat and he is the one that pushed me to take the extra hush money."

Brian's eyes widened. "And you didn't mention this before because…?"

Callum looked at Brian and said, "I don't know, I thought no need to drag more people into it, I just figured he was paid off too and we wouldn't need him. But the more we talk about it I can see he is a piece we would need."

Brian shook his head as if disappointed but resolved to get on with it, he says, "So the other boat was Angus's boat, okay. Did Angus just show up? Wait, was the crash planned, I mean did you know about it before it happened, what's going on here Callum?"

Callum looked at them questioningly for a moment, "What? No, no plan, of course not. Why would I plan on my boat getting pummeled and maybe me dying in the process? What the fuck guys?"

Everyone nodded their heads agreeing yes that wouldn't make sense but seemed like none of this made sense.

"Angus? Isn't that — Mabel's new husband's nephew," Brian said. "Okay so now the Angus info is not so surprising, and definitely confirms we are in the right direction."

Brodie nodded, his eyes intense. "Aye, but he's a dodgy one. We'll need to be clever." He scratched his beard, "What if we let slip about the footage? Rattle him a bit?"

Eilish asked Brian, "How dodgy, would you say he is babe?"

Brian turned to look at Eilish, "Oh no,no,no, that's a terrible idea."

Brodie and Callum stop talking and look at Brian and Eilish, Brodie asks, "What's a terrible idea? Hey, any idea at this point is bloody great if you ask me. You're being a bit harsh aren't ye? You haven't even heard it yet; you should have some faith in your woman there Brian."

"Shut up Brodie," Brian snapped. "She wants to flirt with Andrew and get info, not a good idea at all, really bad."

Brodie stammers, "Oh right, of course, but wait that's not that bad an…." Brodie sees Brian's face and changes course, "No, no you're right, terrible idea."

Callum voices his concern, "I have my doubts about him, Eilish. If he discovered what was going on while you were with him... I don't think he can be trusted. Let's keep brainstorming."

"Guys," Eilish says with a smile, "It will be okay, you are all so sweet but honestly it would be fine. I can bump into him somewhere and arrange to meet where there are other people, or you lot can follow us or something."

Brodie suggests, "It's a good idea, but maybe we can use it in a different way. He's not going to open up to someone he just met, even if that someone is as amazing as you, Eilish. How about distracting him while one of us sneaks into his office?"

Brian says, "Lads this is not some movie, you can't just sneak into his office, there are people everywhere. And we have no idea when he would be there or what to look for."

Callum jumps into the chatter and says, "I know what we are looking for."

The three turn and put all their attention on Callum, "His briefcase, he takes that thing absolutely everywhere."

Immediately Brian is thinking, '*How does Callum know that?*' but he keeps his thoughts to himself.

"So, we have to get a hold of his briefcase," Brian ponders out loud. "Maybe this could be a movie moment, we find out what kind of case he has, get the same one and switch them out."

Eilish says, "I kinda like it, my love. Look it's something to start with, what about the nephew?"

Brodie says, "He is gone, I saw him the day of the crash and haven't seen him since."

Callum says, "Okay so briefcase it is, how and when do we do the switcheru?"

Brian says, "Listen lads, I'm exhausted, I'm going to go and have a chat with Mum see what she can come up with and we can take it from there. But at least now we have some sort of plan. We need that Briefcase." Brian and Eilish hold hands and head to the bike shed. Leaving Brodie and Callum to go back and forth with ideas.

Brodie yells out to Brian, "See you in the morning, let us know what she says."

Brian and Eilish wave as they leave the dock to ride along the coastline towards home.

Chapter 14

Callum and the 'people'

rian and Eilish arrive home, relieved to unload their shoes and coats. As they enter the living room, they see Jan dozing in her armchair by the warm fire. They slide by Jan, quickly tip-toing towards their bedroom, whispering what they are going to do to each other. Eilish lets out a squeal as Brian playfully pinches her butt, then just as they start to open the bedroom door, Jan calls out.

"Brian, is that you? Come here to me a minute, I have to tell ye something."

Eilish and Brian stopped in their stride, looked at each other in a silent,'*do we pretend we didn't hear her and continue on with our plan of ripping each other's clothes off or do we come to our senses and know that Jan knows very well we heard her.*'

In unison they let out their held breath, turn around and head to the living room.

"Hey, Mum, sorry did we wake ye? Actually, I'm glad you're awake we have a couple of questions."

"Aye, and I think I may have the answers. You go first with your questions." Jan said.

"Okay so we know Angus is involved which again leads us to Mabel and Andrew. We knew about Mabel but now it's getting deeper and deeper, we need proof, somehow, about their involvement. Proof without turning Callum in. He thinks, and I agree, they will just deny anything he says. He can't afford to get into that battle."

Jan is nodding her head, not surprised by anything her son is telling her, she knows all this. Or felt she did but it was good to get validated. She could have more trust in her visions now.

Jan sat up and said, "Son, you're right about the briefcase, you have to get a hold of that somehow."

Brian cut her off, "You had another vision, what was it, what did you see?"

Jan continues, "People, about six people, not from around here and not fishermen. Two women and a child and three men, somehow all connected to Callum. They are at his house."

Eilish and Brian look at each other in puzzlement. Brian knows Callum and he is not the type to have a group of strangers over to his house.

"At his house now? We just left Callum, why didn't he say anything?"

Jan sits back, "That's what you have to find out lad, see what is going on there and this mess will make more sense. Okay so, I'm off to bed. You two should get some sleep too, it's late. We can talk more in the morning about getting our hands on that briefcase, goodnight." Jan got up, put her teacup in the kitchen sink, gave Brian a kiss on his forehead and shuffled off to her bedroom.

Eilish and Brian sat in silence until Brian finally said, "Fuck, what is going on here, Callum is having secret parties at his house while the Mrs. is away? If you knew Callum the way I do," Brian just shook his head in bewilderment, "Ridiculous, no way."

Brian and Eilish shower and finally get to make love. This trip has brought them closer than either of them thought possible. They have been through stressful, risky, and frustrating experiences, and have felt the satisfaction of overcoming those emotions together.

They supported each other and laughed with each other in perfect timing and harmony. All this flow edged into their love making, creating the ultimate bonding of two people meant to be together forever. There is a mutual silent understanding of equal, overwhelming love for each other. It is the freest feeling each of them have ever experienced.

While Eilish and Brian are sleeping, Brian gets a text.

~

Brodie's boots crunched on the gravel path as he rounded the corner, the salty sea air ruffling his thick beard. He stopped short. There was Callum, emerging from the fish & chipper with a mountain of greasy paper parcels.

"Jings, that's a lot of chips," Brodie muttered under his breath.

Callum glanced around furtively "Oh there ye are Brodie." Callum see's Brodie questioning the amount of chips. "I know, I'm bloody starving and sure I can have some for the breakfast too."

"Oh, true that Callum, ye could I suppose. Have ye heard of cornflakes or toast even? Very popular these days for the morning meal. And don't forget those egg things, oh God Callum, do you not know how to fry an egg? You better get that Mrs. back sooner than later there boyo, before you turn into a lump of lard. Well goodnight, Callum, I'll see ye in the morning."

Callum laughed at Brodie's sarcasm, nodded goodnight and turned the corner towards home.

Brodie continued up the road towards his place but then he paused, thought for a second and turned around. He trailed Callum at a distance, ducking behind a parked car when his friend looked back. Finally at

Callum's cottage, Brodie crouched in the shadows of a gnarled oak tree. He watched Callum fumble with his keys, nearly dropping the tower of chip parcels.

"C'mon, man," Callum hissed. "Get it together."

The door clicked shut. Brodie crept closer, pulse pounding in his ears. Skirting the edge of the property, Brodie approached the back of the house. His foot caught on a root, and he stumbled, barely catching himself.

"Shite!" he whispered fiercely.

Brodie pressed his back against the rough stone wall, straining his ears. What was he even looking for? He shook his head, feeling foolish. But then...

A muffled thump from inside. Hushed voices.

Brodie's eyes widened. Something was definitely amiss with his old friend. But what?

Brodie inched towards the nearest window, his heart hammering against his ribs. A flicker of movement caught his eye. He crouched lower, peering through the gap in the curtains.

"What in the blazes? I knew he was acting off!" he muttered.

Callum's burly form moved across the room, distributing the parcels of chips. He wasn't alone. Shadowy figures huddled in corners, reaching out with trembling hands to accept the food.

Brodie's jaw dropped. "Ah cannae believe it," he whispered in shock.

He counted quickly. One, two, three... six people crammed into Callum's tiny living room. Their clothes were ragged, faces gaunt and fearful.

"Immigrants," Brodie breathed, the realization hitting him like a punch to the gut.

Inside, Callum's voice drifted through the thin glass. "Eat up, lads. We'll move soon."

A woman's voice, barely audible: "Thank you."

Brodie was deeply concerned. What should he do? Confront Callum? His childhood friend was harboring illegal immigrants, but why? First the boat and now this. Does he think he is in the wild west?

He pressed closer, straining to hear more. His boot scraped against the stone path.

Callum's head snapped towards the window.

Brodie ducked, heart in his throat. "Shite, shite, shite," he hissed, scrambling backwards.

The night air bit into Brodie's skin as he crouched behind a scraggly bush, safe distance but getting full view of Callum's front door. Hours had crawled by each minute stretching like toffee.

Finally, the door creaked open. Callum's hefty silhouette emerged, glancing furtively left and right. He whispered urgently, "Coast's clear. Move, now!"

Shadows detached from the darkness, huddling figures scurrying towards a battered van parked in the driveway. Brodie's breath caught as he counted: one, two, three...a child, two women and three men, six people!

Brodie steadied himself against an old fence, raising the phone. Click. The first photo captured what looked like a mother and child but barely visible in the low light. He crept closer, keeping to the shadows.

Callum's voice, low and gruff: "In ye go. Quiet as church mice, mind."

The van's suspension groaned as bodies piled in. Callum slammed the rear doors, then clambered into the driver's seat. The engine sputtered to life.

Brodie had to act fast. *Call someone?* He questioned. His fingers twitched towards his phone; he held back. This was Callum – his mate since boyhood. The lad who'd shared his first pint, who'd kept him together at his da's funeral.

"Ah cannae just..." Brodie muttered, conflicted.

The van's taillights flared red in the gloom as it pulled away. Brodie was half-crouched, keeping to the shadows.

"Ye great eejit," chastising Callum under his breath. Whatever Callum was mixed up in, Brodie knew he had to see it through and find out. But he just didn't want Callum to know he knew, not yet.

Brodie's fingers trembled as he fumbled with his phone, cursing under his breath. "Come on, ye blasted thing," he muttered, activating the camera app. The van's taillights glowed dimly in the distance. He had got a couple of clear pictures.

Brian and Eilish's names highlighted in his contacts. Brodie's thumb hovered over the send button hesitating, a war of loyalty raging within. "Ah Christ, Cal," he whispered, "what've ye gotten yerself into"

With a sharp exhale, he hit send. The message whooshed away, carrying damning evidence against his oldest friend. Brodie's stomach churned, guilt and resolve battling for dominance. He pocketed the phone, eyes fixed on the fading rear lights of Callum's van.

"Forgive me, mate," Brodie murmured, "but this feels bigger than the both of us."

Brodie headed home, exhausted, he fell into bed for a couple of hours sleep before daylight hit.

He woke up to a text from Brian, "Coming over."

Brodie heard a knock on the door.

As soon as Brodie unlatched the door, Brian and Eilish burst through it with energy.

Brian announced, "So it's either immigrants or stowaways and we think stowaways."

"Good morning to you too, ye got my text then?" Brodie said as he filled the kettle with water for tea. "What do ye think he is up to? It's not like him to do anything with people more of a fish guy."

"Come on get dressed, we have to go over there," Brian said.

"Ah come on Brian, can't it wait till a man has his morning tea for god's sake?" Brodie stalling the inevitable, even though he could tell by Brian and Eilish's faces, nope it could not wait. He turned off the kettle, went to the bedroom and got dressed.

The three biked over to Callum's house, the van was parked back in the driveway. Brian knocked on the door, no answer, he knocked again.

Brodie yelled through the door, "Ey chip man, open up its freezing out here."

Eilish walked around back to knock on the back door, she peeked in the window on her way, she saw Callum sleeping on the couch, "Lads," She called out, "He is sleeping on the couch, over here, out back." Callum still didn't wake up with all the noise.

Brodie said, "He probably just got back and passed out."

Eilish called, "The back door is open," She stepped inside, the other two followed.

Brodie went over to the still sleeping Callum, "Ey laddie," He gave him a shake of his shoulder, "Wake up sleeping beauty."

Callum jolted awake, "What the, what are ye doing here, I thought we were meeting by the docks?"

"We have to talk to you Callum," Brian and Eilish sat down while Brodie went to make tea.

"Aye, what is it?" Callum waking up now rubbing his face with his open palm.

"We know Callum." Brian said.

Callum's face changed, "Know what?"

Brodie walked back in, "We know you didn't eat all those bloody chips by yourself Callum. Now come on, what have you landed yourself into?"

Callum put his head down and his face in his hands, "Ah for fuck's sake, could ye not just mind yer business, this isn't a game. This is people's lives, those people and mine and now probably yours. I didn't tell ye for a reason."

The other three sat and looked at Callum waiting for him to explain.

"Feck it," he said, "Is that kettle on Brodie?"

The kettle whistles and Brodie leaves to finish making the tea.

Chapter 15

Callum tells all

Callum swallowed hard and goes back to the night of the incident. "Okay, so the plan was to meet the tanker, and they would unload stowaways onto my boat."

Eilish said to herself, 'so they were stowaways.' Then she cut Callum off. "Wait a minute though, why didn't they just turn them in at the port if they found them on the boat?"

Brian jumped in, "You can't come into port with stowaways on board, it's not legal."

"Right exactly," Callum agrees, "So anyway, everything was going okay, the sea was calm, I was at the coordinates on time, then I see this bloody tanker coming right at me."

Brodie asks, "Yeah what really happened there, the captain wasn't drunk was he?"

"I'm not sure," Callum says, "I don't think he was drunk; Angus said the stowaways were putting up a fight, maybe he just got distracted. The stowaways told me, 'No fight,' so who knows."

"They probably didn't know what was going on and thought they were getting thrown overboard," Eilish said.

"Yes, could have been that too," Callum agrees, "so the bloody tanker crunches my stern, my engines are now hanging off the back of my boat. With all this wreckage, something damaged the tanker and, hey presto, we have oil leaking out from both my engines and the tanker. Now we are dealing with bloody chaos. I can't take the stowaways; my boat is still floating but obviously not going anywhere. The tanker sends down a dinghy with a couple of divers to fix the oil leak and pick me up at the same time. I'm waiting on the stupid dinghy while the divers are below and next thing I know Angus shows up on his boat. As much as Angus is an idiot, I was happy to see him that night."

"Okay so Angus picks you up, does he know about the stowaways? How did he know your location, did you call him, did you put out a mayday on 16 that he heard or?" asked Brodie.

Callum looks at Brodie like he is an idiot, "Come on Brodie why would I do that, I may as well just walk into jail if I do that, no I had to hope Mabel got my frantic message and come through, and she did, thank God." Callum takes a gulp of his now tepid tea, makes a face and goes on with the story. "So once Angus shows up, he picks me up, the tanker sends another dinghy with the stowaways on it. They board Angus's boat. The divers take both dinghies back to the tanker and we take off, stowaways in hand. Home free right? Wrong."

"Oh God, what happened?" Brian asks, "Always trouble with that Angus fella."

"I was going to bring them to the mainland, and they would go on from there, they had contacts that would take care of them, but we are not on my boat are we…Angus's bloody boat breaks down."

"Oh noooo," Says Eilish, "What did you do?"

Brian and Brodie are sitting staring at Callum as they put themselves in that situation. Silenced by the thought.

"Well, we got one engine working but there were too many people. That boat wasn't going to move with eight people on board and only one working engine. So, the charming Angus says they have to get off."

"Get off, what do you mean, into the water?" asked Eilish shocked.

"He took them to the beach and left them there. I had to go with Angus because he knows feck all about engines and if he broke down again, it would have been bad news."

"So that's why they were at your house." said Brian.

"Of course, what was I going to do just leave them there?"

Brian and Brodie sat back satisfied from getting a clearer picture but also in deep thought of what to do next.

Brian shook his head slowly. "Jesus, Callum. Do you have any idea how much trouble you could be in if you were caught?"

"I know. I never meant..." Callum's voice broke. Fear coiled in his gut.

Brodie stood abruptly, his chair scraping against the floor. "Where are they now, Cal? The stowaways?"

Eilish thought she saw something out of the corner of her eye by the window, but she put it down to being on edge. She went back into the conversation.

"Safe. I got them to the mainland. They had connections there. But no one else can know. If anyone finds out I told you..." Callum met each of their eyes in turn, desperation rising like bile in his throat. "Please, you can't tell anyone else. Ever."

Silence hung heavy in the air. Callum searched his friends' faces for some sign of understanding of the precariousness of the situation. He saw shock and fear, mirroring his own. Yes, he thought, they get it.

Then Brian held up a hand to keep the group quiet. He crept towards the window, his movements slow and deliberate. The others watching Brian, glanced over at each other, as he inched closer to the glass.

Outside, Andrew stood perfectly still, his ear pressed against the window frame. He had heard Callum tell them everything. The stowaways, Callum's involvement, the tangled web of secrets. "That bloody Callum, I knew he wasn't to be trusted, why does everyone on this island have a big mouth?" Andrew muttered.

Brian was on high alert, adrenaline coursing through his veins. He knew someone was out there, but who? And what did they want? His mind scanned the possibilities, each more terrifying than the last.

Suddenly, a twig snapped beneath Andrew's foot, the sound echoing like a gunshot in the stillness of the night. "Shit." Andrew whispered as he quickly scurried away.

For a moment, time stood still. Brian, Brodie and Callum bolted outside but as quickly as they had heard the noise, Andrew vanished into the darkness, melting away like a ghost. By the time they got out there; nothing, just quiet with the odd countryside noise. Brian stumbled back inside, his face pale. "Whoever that was, he heard everything."

The other three followed and sat back down. Time to plan what to do next.

"Here is the thing, if that was Andrew or Angus or anyone really, and they find out I told you lot about all this, then it's going to get dangerous." Callum said. "For me and you. We have to keep this between us. Brian, I'm sure Jan knows already, so let's say keep it between the five of us." Callum continues, "Andrew and Mabel are deep into this as far as I can make out. That tanker had been floating idle for a few weeks due to the stowaways on board. But since the price of oil had plummeted, the company didn't see it as a pressing issue. But now that the price has skyrocketed, they want to capitalize on the situation and have paid Andrew and Mabel handsomely to get rid of the stowaways and let them, now legally, come into port."

Brian stood abruptly, pacing the small room. "This is insane. Mabel and Andrew, mixed up with smuggling stowaways? And you..." He whirled to face Callum, anger flashing in his eyes. "You helped them?"

Callum flinched, shame washing over him that came out in anger. "I didn't know what else to do Brian! First of all, what choice did I have... hardly any fishing and when I do catch, I can't pay the fecking processing and packing fees plus the taxes, I nearly end up owing them money. I was in the negative Brian. Second of all, I couldn't just leave them there, on that beach. They were desperate, scared. They would have gone to jail or been sent back. I had to do something."

Eilish stepped between them, her hands raised. "Enough. This isn't helping. We need to focus on what to do next."

Brodie nodded, his expression grim. "Eilish is right. We can't change what's already happened. But we can decide what we do from here."

Eilish leaned forward, "why didn't you tell us, Callum? We could have helped, we could have..."

"No," Callum interrupted, shaking his head vehemently. "I couldn't risk it. I couldn't put all of ye in danger."

Brian's brow furrowed, his mind attempting to rationalize the implications of Callum's deeds. The stowaways, the oil tanker, Mabel and Andrew... it was a tangled web of secrets and lies, and they were all caught in the middle.

Brodie shifted uncomfortably in his seat. "But what about now, Callum? What if they come looking for them and then for you?"

Callum's shoulders sagged, the weight of his actions pressing down on him. "I don't know. I thought I was doing the right thing, but now... I just don't know."

Eilish reached out, placing a comforting hand on Callum's arm. "We'll figure this out, Callum."

Brian and Brodie exchanged a glance, a silent understanding passing between them. They were in deep, far deeper than they wanted to be. The consequences of Callum's actions, of Mabel and Andrew's schemes, could be devastating.

Callum buried his face in his hands, his voice muffled. "This is all my fault. I never should have gotten involved. And now I've put ye all in danger."

Brodie shook his head, his voice firm. "No, Callum. You did what you thought was right and what ye had to do. And now, well now, we are going to figure out how to fix this."

Brian nodded, his mind turning with possibilities. They had to act fast, before Andrew turned on them.

"Okay, listen, we need a plan. We are pretty sure Andrew knows we know. So, we have to get to him before he gets to us."

~

The pub bustled with its usual crowd, the warm glow of the lights casting shadows on the weathered wooden tables. Brian's fingers drummed against his whiskey glass, the amber liquid untouched. Eilish's gaze darted between the door and the clock on the wall, her brow furrowed.

"He should be here by now," She murmured, her voice tinged with concern.

Brodie leaned forward, his elbows resting on the table. "Give him a few more minutes. He will be here."

Brian's mind replaying the conversation from earlier. The weight of the secret they now carried seemed to press down on him, suffocating. He took a sip of his whiskey, the warmth coursing through his body doing little to calm his nerves.

Minutes ticked by, each one feeling like an eternity. The door swung open, and their heads snapped up, only to be disappointed by the sight of a stranger.

"Something's wrong," Brian said, his voice low. "Callum wouldn't just not show up."

Eilish nodded, her fingers twisting the napkin in her lap. "What if Andrew..." She trailed off, unable to finish the thought.

Brian nodding his head in agreement, "Finish up, we have to go and find him. Now."

They pushed back from the table, Brodie gulped down the rest of his pint while Eilish and Brian abandon their drinks.

"Well hold on, for God's sake," Brodie mumbled as he contemplated slamming back Brian's drink and then thought better of it.

Eilish and Brian are already out the door into the starkly contrasting cold, still night. Brodie burst through the door seconds behind them.

"Oh God it's cold," Brodie gasped as he quickly put on his jacket, not bothering to zip it up but grabbing both sides to wrap in close with his folded arms

"We split up," Brian said, his voice steady despite the fear that gripped him. "I'll, check his house. Eilish, the docks. Brodie take the beach. If you find anything, call straight away."

They nodded.

As they went their separate ways, Brian's mind whirled with possibilities. The stowaways, Andrew's involvement, Mabel's role in it all - the pieces were falling into place, but the picture they formed was far from clear.

All he knew was that they had to act fast. Before it was too late. Before the price they paid for their loyalty to Callum became too high to bear.

The door to Callum's house stood ajar, an eerie stillness hanging in the air. Brian started sweating in places he didn't know was possible, like the backs of his knees. He pushed open the door, the creak of the hinges shattering the silence. "Callum?" His voice echoed through the empty rooms, unanswered.

He moved cautiously, his eyes scanning for any sign of disturbance. The living room was untouched, a half-empty mug of tea on the table, a book lying open on the arm of the chair. But as he stepped into the kitchen, his breath caught in his throat.

Blood. So much blood. It pooled on the floor, smeared across the cabinets, a violent splash of crimson against the stark white tiles. And there, in the center of it all, lay Callum, unconscious. He stumbled back, then got to his knees, hands shaking as he fumbled for a pulse, Brian reached for his phone. "Eilish," he choked out when she answered. "It's Callum. He's...in bad shape, he has a pulse, but really bad."

The words felt foreign on his tongue. He sank to the floor and called 999 for an ambulance. His back against the wall and Callum's head on his lap, the reality of it all crashed over him.

The ambulance had just pulled in before Eilish arrived then Brodie showed up close behind on his bike. They stood in the driveway for a second questioning what had happened, then Eilish bolted up to the house. Brodie called out her name after he tried to grab her, but she was too fast. He didn't want her to walk in on what he suspected was a gory mess.

As Eilish got to the front door she saw the foot of the stretcher with Callum's covered feet being rolled out first. One medic pushing and one holding the oxygen over Callum's beaten face. Brian was following behind getting info on his condition and what hospital he would be taken to. Eilish stood at the door watching poor Callum get maneuvered into the ambulance. She waited for Brian to fill them in on how he was. Brian stood watching the ambulance leave, then he put his hands in his face and shook his head.

"FUCK!," He let the 'fuck' escape from the depths of his despair.

Eilish felt his pain, she went to him and put her hand on his shoulder, Brian turned and melted into her, she just held him.

Brian broke away took a deep breath, started to get down to business, Eilish stopped him.

"Hold on there Mr., how is he, what did they say?"

"Oh sorry, yes let's go inside to Brodie."

Brodie was sitting on the couch, in slight shock. As soon as Brian and Eilish walked in his eyes woke up.

"So how is he, is he alright, will he be alright?"

"They don't know, but definitely a few broken bones," Brian said simply. "We will just have to wait and see. Callum is tough, I don't think this is going to be what gets him."

Brodie nodded his head in agreement, then let out a low but very determined, growl, "I will fucking kill the bastard that done this," He raised his head and looked directly at Brian and emphasized, "Fucking kill him!"

Brian nodded his head in agreement, more to calm Brodie down, he knew Brodie meant it and now Brian's job was to make sure that didn't happen. Brian wanted justice, for sure but that would be in revenge not murder. Brodie landing himself in jail for murder would not be a satisfying end to all this.

"We have to get the briefcase before he dumps it. By the time the police get to him it could be days and it will be well gone by then." Brian says

Brodie nodded; his fists clenched at his sides. "I'm in."

Eilish took a shuddering breath, the weight of their decision settling on her shoulders. She knew the risks, the danger they were walking into. But she also knew that they had no choice.

Chapter 16

The truth

Brian's fingers hovered over his phone. He took a deep breath, then typed:

Andrew. I know what you've done. Meet me at the dock, 8 PM. Bring 100k if you want my silence. Otherwise, I go to the police. Send. *No turning back now*, he thought.

Brian slipped his phone into his pocket, doubts setting in, impossible questions with no chance of real supportable answers. Was this too dangerous? Maybe, but he was in too deep to back out now, or so he told himself every time he thought about bailing.

His phone buzzed. Andrew's reply: I will be there, in the meantime, don't do anything stupid.

"Okay it worked," Brian said to himself. "I also think I may have just done something stupid, oh well, it won't be the first time." Brian shook his head at his own brazenness.

Across town, Eilish, crouched in the shadows, eyes fixed on Andrew and Mabel's house. She watched Andrew leave and then stayed to make sure Mabel didn't leave and perhaps walk in on Brodie. The curtains were drawn, but a faint light filtered through into the night.

Eilish shivered, pulling her jacket tighter. "Come on, Mabel," I whispered. "Let me see you." she wanted to be reassured by Mabel's movement, confirm she was still inside the house. I didn't see her leave, but you never know with this slippery one.

Felt like forever, my legs cramped, I was freezing but I didn't dare move. I was far enough away from the house not to be seen. Brian said he would text when he was finished with Andrew. I couldn't help obsessively worry about how that was going.

A car approached. I held my breath as it slowed, then kept going. False alarm.

I checked my watch. 8:05 PM. *Fuck it's happening now*! I thought. *Please be careful*

Movement caught my eye. The front door opened a crack. I tensed up, "Oh shit she is leaving," I started to take out my phone to text Brodie and Brian. But, no need, she was just coming out to walk the dog!

Oh no no, p*lease don't come this way.* I froze and closed my eyes tightly, as if by not seeing them they wouldn't see me. Every so often, I cautiously open a small slit of my right eye to take a peek.

"Whew," I was finally able to exhale, I didn't realize how much air I had trapped inside my body, they were walking the other way. I continued watching, both eyes open, until they went back inside the house.

Bloody hell, that was close, I thought, and noticed I felt a little warmed up now. "That's the trick," I mumbled to myself, "get terrified every 15 mins or so and stay nice and toasty warm."

~

Speaking of terrifying moments, Brodie's heart had a drum kit inside his chest as he slipped into Andrew's office building. The night guard's footsteps echoing down the hallway Brodie ducked behind a potted plant then froze still until the guard passed.

"Bloody hell," he muttered, his Scottish brogue mumbled in a whisper. "This is pure madness."

Crouching low, Brodie scurried towards Andrew's office, his weathered hands steady as he picked the lock. The door clicked open, and he slid inside, closing it softly behind him.

Moonlight streamed through the windows, casting long shadows across the opulent space. Brodie's eyes, now used to the dark, darted around searching for the briefcase.

"C'mon, ye bastard," he growled, opening a closet, "Where are ye hiding?"

A noise in the hallway made him instinctively duck down in place. Footsteps approached, then faded. Brodie gulped, resuming his frantic search.

~

Meanwhile, at the docks, Brian stood alone, straining to see through the darkness for any signs of movement. He checked his watch. 8:05 PM. Where was Andrew?

Out of nowhere a hand clamped over his mouth. Brian struggled, but strong arms pinned him.

"You should've just left it alone, lad," Andrew's voice hissed in his ear.

"*Fuck*," thought Brian. *This wasn't exactly how it was supposed to go, but I did have a feeling it would take a violent turn.* They had all agreed to check in at 8:30pm. If anyone didn't, the other two would be right there to help or find them. Hopefully find them alive. Brian's top priority was giving Brodie time to find the briefcase and then to get away as quickly as possible. Now he was unsure if the, 'getting away,' part, was going to happen but he was relieved when he felt the boat beneath him. They were going into his territory, gave him more of a chance.

They dragged Brian to the stern of the boat, his protests muffled, as they pushed off from the dock.

The boat cut through the waves, the shoreline receding. Brian's stomach churned with dread. Yes, this was his territory, but it still wasn't good, not good at all!

Eilish checked her phone again it was 8:35pm. Okay time to get out of here but why hadn't she heard from either of them. As she pulled her bike out of the bush her phone pinged. It was Brodie, "I'm out, on my way to dock."

Eilish hopped on her bike and pedaled as fast as she could. Between biking in the dark and her adrenaline, it felt like she was practically flying. She slowed down as she got close to their planned meet up spot. She wanted to make sure all was clear.

Brodie came up behind her, "Pisst, hey, over here."

Eilish quickly turned and went to Brodie. "What happened, did you get it, where is Brian?"

Brodie held up the case, "Yep, I got it. In and out like a puff of wind."

"Where is Brian?" Eilish asked again with added panic.

"I was going to ask you; he is not here taking a piss or something."

Eilish was upset now, "What? No, he is not here. Oh God Brodie not again, that man takes way too many risks!"

~

"Well lad, you should have minded your own business." Andrew said, producing a heavy rock and rope.

Brian's blue eyes flashed defiance. "Aye maybe I should have, trust me, I thought that a few times. But the deeper I got in and saw what corrupt bastards you and your wife are, I couldn't help myself."

Andrew nodded to his men. They grabbed Brian, while tying a rock to his ankles, he thrashed wildly, but it was no use.

"Don't think this is the end, you fuck" Brian gasped.

Andrew smirked. "Well, it definitely is the end for you, my friend."

With a shove, Brian plummeted into the icy water, sinking fast. The surface grew distant, panic clawing at his chest.

As darkness closed in, one thought burned in Brian's mind: *Eilish. He had to survive.*

Brian heard the boat above, kick into gear and take off then, darkness. Cold. Pressure.

Brian's lungs screamed for air as he sank deeper. The weight around his ankles dragged him down relentlessly. His fingers clawed at the ropes, desperate for release.

A flash of movement. Sleek bodies circled him.

Dolphins?

Intelligent eyes met his. A seal joined them, its whiskers twitching.

Brian's vision blurred. His chest ached.

Suddenly, teeth tugged at the ropes. The seal and dolphins worked in tandem, their movements precise. Brian felt the bonds loosening.

Free.

He kicked hard, propelling himself upward. The animals flanked him, guiding his ascent.

Brian broke the surface with a gasp, gulping air greedily. "Thank you," he wheezed, clinging to a dolphin's dorsal fin.

~

Miles away, Jan Maclean bolted upright in her chair. Her eyes, unfocused, saw beyond the cozy Scottish cottage.

"Brian," she whispered, her voice trembling.

Jan's gaze snapped to urgency. "He's in danger," she mumbled. "Andrew... he's done something terrible."

~

Brodie looked down at the dock and saw Jan. That was weird for her to be out here at this hour. Brodie elbowed Eilish to look down at the dock, "It's Jan."

Eilish didn't think and immediately ran down the hill towards Jan, "Jan! Jan!" Eilish called.

Jan turned and held out her arms, when Eilish finally reached her, they were both shaking.

"We can't find Brian," Eilish exclaimed.

"Aye I know child, he is out there," Jan looked over EIlish's shoulder, "Come on Brodie, get yer boat, I'll explain on the way." The engine of Brodie's boat roared to life, cutting through the night air. Eilish gripped the railing, eyes scanning the dark waters.

"We need to head northwest," Jan shouted over the wind, her gray hair whipping around her face. "I can feel him."

Brodie nodded, his weathered hands steady on the wheel. "You had a vision, Jan?"

Eilish's stomach churned, matching the choppy waves.

"I did. Can't say for certain where he is out here," Jan replied, her brow furrowed in concentration. "But he's out here and alive. I know that much."

The boat lurched as Brodie increased speed. Eilish stumbled, catching herself on a nearby seat.

"Sorry, lass," Brodie called out. "Time's not on our side."

Eilish nodded, her throat tight. She scanned the horizon, desperate for any sign of Brian. The vastness of the ocean seemed to mock her efforts.

"There!" Jan's cry pierced the air. "Look!"

Eilish's heart leapt as she spotted a dark shape in the water, moving unnaturally fast. As they drew closer, she gasped.

Brian, clinging to a dolphin's fin, his head barely above water.

"Brian!" Eilish shouted, her voice cracking.

He looked up, relief washing over his exhausted features. "Eilish!"

Brodie maneuvered the boat alongside Brian, put the boat in neutral, then joined Eilish and Jan to reach down and haul him aboard. Brian collapsed on the deck, coughing and shivering.

Eilish wrapped her arms around him, tears streaming down her face. "I thought I'd lost you, again." she whispered.

Brian managed a weak smile. "Can't get rid of me yet, girl."

Jan's eyes glistening. "I'm so relieved you're okay son but you're a bloody eejit, do you know that? I raised a mad man."

Brian laughed while giving Jan a hug, "Aye you have that, I could have done with the ole seal skin out there tonight, Mum."

Brodie wrapped Brian in one of those foil blankets he had in the cockpit. Then he turned the boat towards shore. Eilish held Brian close, listening to his steady heartbeat. She glanced at the water, catching a glimpse of a dolphin's fin before it disappeared beneath the waves.

Brodie's weathered hands reached for the briefcase. He thrust it towards Brian, a grin splitting his bearded face. "Ye won't believe what I've got for ye, mate."

Brian's eyes widened. He reached out, fingers trembling. "Is that...?"

"Aye, the very one." Brodie's voice dropped to a conspiratorial whisper. "Nabbed it right from under Andrew's nose."

Brian, an unusual shade of purple from the cold, managed to let a smile crease across his mouth. He could relax a bit now.

"Brodie, we..." Brian's voice caught. He swallowed hard, "We did it." Then he whispered, "Callum?"

The high of their achievement was brought back to reality with the memory of Callum's almost death.

"Don't know yet," Brodie yelled over the engines. "We will ring the hospital when we get back."

Brian nodded; his grip tightened on the case. "We did it," he breathed. "At least both of our near-death experiences won't be for nothing." He smiled.

He had faced death again tonight but saved by his ocean allies. He was okay, and that damn Andrew won't know what hit him.

"So," Eilish said, "What's our next move?"

Jan put her hand up, "What's next is we go home to our beds! We will have a clear head in the morning to figure out the next step."

Brodie pulled the boat up close to the beach by Jan's house to let Brian get off with the briefcase. They didn't want to bump into his captors at the dock and reveal to Andrew he failed to finish his mission of murder.

Chapter 17

Escape and what to do

s Eilish was the first one off the boat, she grabbed the lines to tie off before the boat had a chance to drift into its neighbor. The dock creaked under her feet waiting for Jan and Brodie to jump off. Sailboats and fishing boats bobbed in the grey water, masts stark against the overcast sky. No sign of Andrew or his men. Hopefully they went home thinking they had a successful night.

Brodie's eyes darted from vessel to vessel back to the shore. "I dinnae like this, Jan, come on let's go."

Jan placed a hand on his arm. "Hush now, lad. We're safe for the moment."

Eilish glanced at Jan, marveling at her calmness. How composed she was when danger lurked around every corner. But then, Jan was no ordinary woman.

"Brodie is right, hurry up, let's get out of here," Eilish whispered, "I mean, before they show up or something."

"Aye, okay, okay," Jan said, focusing on Brodie. "Come back with us, dear. It's not safe for you to be alone."

Brodie thought for a second, "Aye, right so."

"We'll be fine," Jan assured him. "We just need to stick together now. Alright, let's away."

As they turned to leave, Eilish quickened her pace, she wanted to get out of there and be with Brian.

Jan's voice cut through her spiraling fears. "Eilish, love. Breathe. Come on, let's get the bikes. Brodie, I think you should drive," Jan gave a glance towards Eilish, Brodie nodded his head in agreement and understanding.

The wind whipped Eilish's chestnut hair as she sat behind Brodie, clinging onto his waist. Her backside digging into the carrier rack and her legs aching from holding her feet away from the wheels. Jan kept pace beside them, surprisingly spry for her age.

As they skidded to a stop, Eilish's legs wobbled when they hit solid ground, she glanced over at Jan before stumbling towards the door, her legs cramping.

"He's inside," Jan assured her. "Safe."

Inside, Brian hunched by the fireplace, papers strewn around him. Intense with concentration he snapped up as they entered.

"Eilish," he breathed, relief evident in his slight Scottish brogue, well compared to Brodie's and Jan's, it was slight. "I was worried sick."

Eilish crossed the room, collapsing beside him. "What have you found?"

"It's just as we thought. Look at this." Brian said.

He thrust a document into her hands. Eilish's eyes widened as she scanned the contents, "What the.," she looked up at Brian in disbelief. He nodded his head in assurance that what she was seeing was correct.

"The oil spill, stowaways, Callum's involvement...they meant to kill him?" she whispered. "It's all here. Everything, holy crap!"

A sharp knock at the door cut her off. Everyone froze, exchanging panicked glances.

Eilish's stomach dropped to her ankles. Had Andrew found them already? Was this the end?

Brodie moved swiftly, positioning himself between the door and the others, muscles tensing beneath his worn fisherman's sweater.

"I'll handle this," he growled, his accent thickening with tension.

Jan's eyes darted to Brian, a silent communication passing between mother and son. Jan's eyes said, "Not to worry."

Eilish gathered the papers, stuffing them back into the briefcase with trembling hands. Ready to fight and hide at the same time.

The knocking intensified, more insistent now.

Brian put his arm around Eilish, his voice low and steady. "It's okay."

"Hush," Jan interrupted, her eyes slightly unfocused. "It's not Andrew. But we're not out of danger yet."

Brodie cautiously approached the door, his broad frame tense. He cracked it open, peering out.

"It's Morag?" he announced, relief evident in his voice but lingered with question, "Andrew's housekeeper."

The petite, grey-haired woman slipped inside, her face etched with worry. "You need to move, now," She hissed. "Andrew will be on his way soon, he is figuring it out."

Eilish's blood ran cold. *So, no death sentences this time but can we trust this woman?* She thought.

"No time," Morag insisted. "Go on now get to the mainland, go on away with ye. I have to get back."

Brian stood; decision made. "Right. We leave in five minutes." He looked around to make sure Eilish got all the papers safely back in the briefcase. At the last minute he grabbed the seal skin, just in case.

Brodie announced, "You head down to the beach, I'm going to go and get the boat, I will meet ye there. It's too risky If we all go to the dock."

The late-night cold air bit at Eilish's cheeks as she quickly, carefully, eyes down, put one foot in front of the other. Almost floating with fear as they navigated down the dark rocky path to the shore. They could see Brodie's boat's wake in the distance.

After Brodie dropped the anchor he made his way to the stern of the boat, calling out in a hushed tone to his soon to be passengers to be careful. "There are unexpected rocks sticking out of the bottom sand." He cautioned.

We waded through the freezing, shallow water towards his boat. Brian carefully holding the briefcase above his head and clutching his seal skin under his arm. Jan and I had a bag of clothes each and some towels. Brodie extended his rough hand to assist us onto the boat. After everyone was on board, Brian pulled up the anchor and Brodie started the engine. Brian slid next to Eilish, his arm protective around her shoulders. "You okay?" He murmured.

She nodded, not trusting her voice. The realty solidly hitting her in the face… she was scared. These were murderers after them, ruthless.

Jan's voice cut through her spiraling thoughts. We're doing the right thing, dear. Have faith."

The mainland loomed closer, a smudge on the horizon growing more distinct. Eilish's nerves jangled with each nautical mile.

"There!" Brodie shouted suddenly. "Is that.."

A sleek speedboat roared into view, closing fast.

"Andrew," Brian growled.

Eilish's heart hammered. "Can we outrun them?"

Brodie shook his head grimly. "Not in this old girl." He started to slow down.

Brian quickly stripped and got into his seal skin, "Just say you are out here looking for me, say I was seen down by the dock, and you are worried, okay? I will meet you at the shore. Hide that bag they have no idea you have it." Brian slid into the deep ocean off the port bow just seconds before Andrew's boat caught up to them.

As the speed boat leveled up to Brodie's starboard, the captain waved at him to slow down. "What are you lot doing out here at this time of night?"

Brodie leaned towards the speedboat putting his hand to his ear indicating he can't hear the captain. It was Andrew's men not Andrew. They didn't know anything yet.

Brodie turned off his engine and yelled, "Sorry, what did you say?"

The captain repeated, "What are you doing out here?"

"Oh," Said Brodie, "Well I could ask you the same question." Jan gave Brodie a sharp look. "Actually, I'm glad you stopped, we are looking for my friend Brian, he was last seen at the docks, and we can't find him anywhere so thought we would check out here. Have you seen anything bobbing on the water?"

The captain couldn't figure out if Brodie was fucking with them.

The captain responded. "What? no nothing. Why would he be out here?"

Brodie quickly shot back, "His boat has a habit of breaking down at the most inconvenient times so wanted to check. If you see him tell him we are searching for him, thanks."

The captain nodding his head, staring like he is trying to figure out what's really going on. At last, one of the men says to the captain, "Come on let's get out of here." The captain waves to Brodie and turns the boat around.

All three look at each other with faces of we just escaped death. Brodie kicked his boat into full speed towards the mainland.

There was a small old dock that Brian, Callum and Brodie used to use when they took the boat to the mainland. Sure enough there was a big ole seal swimming around when they pulled up. Eilish screamed, "Brian!"

Jan grabbed her arm, "Quiet child, do ye want the world to know we're here?"

Eilish put her hands over her smiling mouth and whispered through her fingers. "Sorry, sorry, but look it's Brian."

Jan realized that keeping Eilish quiet was a bit of a lost cause. Brian waddled on to the shore and proceeded with the transformation back into his naked human form.

Eilish grabbed Brian's cloths and a towel then hopped off the boat, leaving Brodie and, the more than capable Jan, to tie off . Brodie got the briefcase out of its hiding place as they all gathered on the rickety old dock to figure out what to do next.

"We are going to need a car, but a bit late for a car rental at this hour." Brian said.

"What about an Uber?" Eilish piped in. But she wasn't sure if Uber was a thing in this neck of the woods.

Brian turned to look for Brodie but he was already walking up towards the road and on his phone. "Okay so ye know where we are then, the old dock, right? Ten minutes? Perfect, see ye then."

"Who was that?" Brian asked.

"My old girlfriend," Brodie saw Brian's face change to concern, "Don't worry we can trust her."

"There is only one of your girlfriends that I would trust, and she is married now, so who is it?" Brian asked.

Brodie smiled, "Yeah, it's her. She is not married anymore, by the way."

Brian smiled back, "Well good for you, she was good for you, don't fuck it up this time."

"What are ye talking about we are just friends."

"Okay", Brian said. Brian pointed to headlights in the distance. "Let's hope this is your 'friend'…"

Alison, long brown hair, up in a sloppy bun, not heavy not thin, trusting eyes, determined face, pulls up to the stranded four. Brodie leans down to open the front door. As soon as he opens the door, Alison is yelling at him, "Brodie, what the hell are ye doing in the middle of the night out here, I was having one of the best dreams I have had in a while and what happens, you bloody well pull me out of it like a rabbit out of a hat that was cozy and sleeping." Brodie is holding the door not sure if he should get in or not, everyone else is looking at each other waiting for Brodie's lead.

"Well, are you getting in, or did I drive down here just to yell at ye and drive away?"

Brodie jumps in the front followed by Jan, Eilish and Brian getting in the back.

Alison's tone does a 180o when she sees Jan, "Oh god, is that you Jan, oh sure it's lovely to see ye, and there ye are Brian, back for a little holiday is it?" She glances at Eilish nods and smiles. "Right so, where are we going?"

Brodie turns around and looks at his friends in the back, "What's the next move there, people?"

Jan speaks up, "Would you mind if we stayed a little while at your place Alison, just until we figure out the best way to approach this?"

Alison turns her head to Brodie; he is staring at her waiting to hear her response. Alison wants to ask 'why,' but she can tell by Brodie's face that this is heavy stuff, and he can tell her later in private.

Alison announces, "Sure of course ye can, it will be great to catch up."

Jan says, "Aye, it will to be sure. I hear you're doing well with your pottery. The shop is a gold mine, I hear."

Alison says, "You know Jan, I can't believe how well it's doing, and I love doing it, I meet some great people from all over. But you know what," She puts her hand on Brodie's knee, "The best ones are the ones you have known forever."

Brodie is gushing, his eyes light up with warmth.

They turn onto Alison's driveway, leading to a charming cottage surrounded by a lovely garden. Despite the darkness of the night, it's clear that someone has put a lot of time and effort into maintaining and adding to the beauty of a natural rocky space.

Chapter 18

Telling Sarah about Callum

Brodie rang the hospital to see how Callum was but they wouldn't give information unless he was related. Although the hospital was grateful Brodie called because they needed to contact Callum's family. It seems in the shock of the moment Brian gave Callum's cell number to the ambulance.

The crackling fire was a welcome embrace after finally getting out of their cold wet clothes. Eilish huddled close to Brian on the small sofa, their shoulders touching and a heavy blanket over their laps. The weight of what they were about to do pressed down on them all.

Eilish's stomach churned. "How do we even begin to explain something like this?"

The drive to Callum's in laws house where his wife, Sarah, was staying, felt endless. Eilish's mind went through the different explanations of how to tell someone that their love has been beaten to a pulp and almost died. Will she understand? Did she know what Callum was up to? Brian and Brodie know her, so one of them should be the one to explain. If Sarah gives them a chance, that is, before it all sinks in and she falls apart.

Brian parked the car. No one moved.

"Ready?" Alison asked softly.

They weren't. But they had to be.

Eilish's legs felt like lead as they walked to the front door. Brodie knocked, the sound echoing in the quiet street.

The door opened. Callum's father-in-law opened the door.

"Hey guys, wow Brian long time no see, come in, come in."

The group looked at each other with glances of, 'oh no, they don't know yet.'

Brodie cleared his throat. "Mr. McGregor, can I speak with you for a second…?"

Sarah's showed up behind her dad all smiles. "No way, so good to see ye, God Brian it's been forever. Are we having an impromptu party?" Sarah turned to her dad, "Dad I might have to kick you and Mum out." Sarah laughed. "Come in, come in, let's go into the kitchen."

She took a step back, allowing them to enter the peaceful kitchen where the scent of dinner, having been cleaned up just moments before, still lingered.

Sarah went to fill the kettle for tea. "Ye must be freezing out and about in this cold, where is that Callum fella anyway?" She walked back out into the hall, almost bumping into her dad and Brodie still in the hallway.

Brodie was getting up the courage to break the news but her dad, sensing something was wrong, was getting impatient, "What is it Brodie?" her dad asked softly.

Everyone in the kitchen still standing silently looking at each other. Sarah stopped in mid pace looked at Brodie and her dad, turned to go back into the kitchen finally taking in the aura of her guests. She steadied herself by leaning on the back of one of the kitchen chairs. Brian quickly grabbed her before her legs gave out.

She mumbled, "Is he okay? Please tell me he is okay, injured in the hospital, but okay?" Brian nodded his head. Sarah asked, "Oh God, how bad is he, what happened, is it something with the engine, did the prop catch him?" Sarah put her face in her hands. "I knew it, I knew it, Brian. I told him to be more careful and to take on a mate, we would figure it out, he has to do everything himself."

Brian leaned forward, his voice gentle. "Sarah, Callum was beaten up badly. We found him at the house. We believe it was because he knew too much about what was going on with the tankers and because he was trying to help stowaways."

The silence stretched, heavy and suffocating.

"Where is he now?" asked Sarah not really wanting to hear other details

Brodie walked in from the hall, "At the hospital in Oban," Brian said. Just then the phone rang. Sarah's dad ran to get it before his wife. Sarah went out after her dad and grabbed the phone from him. We heard her talking, we waited.

"What, yes this is his wife Sarah, is he okay?" There was a pause. We read Sarah's reaction. She looked up at us and gave a slight smile with a nod. He was okay.

Sarah hung up the phone she looked up, her face a mask of pain, relief and disbelief.

"They said he is sleeping and needs to rest so I will go in and see him by myself, Dad can you and Mum mind the kids?"

Her dad reached out to hold her as Sarah sobbed. This was not expected, and it felt like she was at the end of her rope. Sarah pushed away from her dad, dried her face and turned to us.

"So, listen lads can you stay for a cup a tea before I go, I just want to catch up a bit?" Sarah turned to her dad, "Thanks dad, can you just give us a minute, don't tell Mum yet, I can't deal with her yet."

We all shuffled back into the kitchen.

Sarah closed the door and asked in a low restrained calm voice, "What the fuck happened?"

"He was trying to protect everyone," Brodie's words flooded out. "In the end he wanted out and was trying to help. He was hiding stowaways until he could get them to the…"

Sarah broke in, "Slow down, what, stowaways? He was hiding stowaways, he wanted out of what, what are you going on about Brodie?"

Brian continued, "Yes, I know it sounds crazy but you need to know he was trying to do the right thing and it all just went wrong. A tanker crashed into Callum's boat and the deal got all messed up. In the end he did the right thing, that's what's important. The people he was doing the job for found out he told us and that he wanted out, so they had to stop him from exposing them."

Sarah's eyes said it all. Callum may get beaten up a bit more. if he isn't careful. "That's enough, I don't want to hear anymore." Sarah left the room leaving us awkwardly standing around. We heard her yell, "I'll be back later Mum." The front door slammed behind her.

We looked at each other knowing that was our cue to file out of the kitchen. Sarah's Mum and Dad came out of the living room just before we got to the front door.

"Oh lads, well isn't it great to see ye, where did that Sarah go without a word?"

We nodded and smiled as Sarah's dad put his hand on his wife's shoulder. She turned to him and saw his face, she immediately asked, "What's happened?"

We left.

~

Eilish's hands trembled as she fed the damning documents into the ancient copier at Alison's. The machine wheezed and groaned, spitting out duplicates with agonizing slowness.

"Hurry up," Brian muttered, peering out the window. "We don't know who might show up." Brodie's voice was grim.

The copier finally finished. Eilish gathered the warm papers, their weight both comforting and terrifying. "Now what?"

Brian ran a hand through his hair. "It's not that simple. The local police.."

"—might be in Andrew's pocket," Eilish finished his sentence.

"Exactly," Brian nodded. "We can't trust anyone here."

"Obviously those people won't hesitate to shut us up," Eilish said, her voice surprisingly calm. "I hope Callum is safe in the hospital."

She lowered her voice and posed another possibility, "But what if they don't believe us?"

"I feel like we're walking into the lion's den," Brian muttered.

"Yep," Eilish agreed, "The lion's den, fed to the sharks, bullet in the head. Whatever is waiting for us I don't think it's going to be a 'good for you,' pat on the back, that's for sure. At least not for a while, but what choice do we have?"

~

The station's glass doors slid open with a hiss. Warm air washed over them, carrying the scent of disinfectant and stale coffee. A bored-looking officer glanced up from the front desk.

"Can I help you?"

Eilish stepped forward, her voice steadier than she felt. "We need to speak with someone about a case of corporate fraud and... an assault."

The officer's eyebrows shot up. "Is that right? Now are these two things connected or should we start with the assault?" The officer dismissively told the group to take a seat, "Someone will be with ye in a minute."

He reached for the phone, speaking in hushed tones.

Minutes crawled by, Eilish's palms grew slick with sweat, her armpits weren't much better. Finally, a door opened, and a stern-faced detective emerged.

"I'm Detective Inspector Wallace. Follow me."

As they filed into a small, windowless room, Eilish not sure if this was the right thing to do but this was it. No turning back now.

Detective Wallace's piercing gaze swept over them. "Now then, what's this about fraud and assault?"

Eilish took a deep breath and began to speak, praying they were doing the right thing.

~

Alison's cottage creaked and groaned in the wind; every sound amplified by their frayed nerves. Eilish peered through a gap in the heavy curtains, scanning the empty street for any sign of suspicious activity.

"See anything?" Brian's voice was low.

Eilish shook her head. "All clear. For now."

Alison bustled in, "I've locked every door and window, just in case." Her Scottish lilt carried a hint of forced cheerfulness.

Headlights appeared on the ceiling from outside, Brodie was up by the window in a flash and then reported back to an alert anxious group.

"It's okay, it's Sarah."

Alison quickly went to the door to let her in.

"Well, don't you lot look like a happy bunch, what's going on? You could cut the air with a blunt knife." Sarah said with a lightness they were not expecting.

"So?" Brian questioned, "How is he?"

Sarah removed her coat and kicked off her shoes, not wanting to track any dirt or water from outside into the house. The rain had just begun.

"He is going to be okay, for now, but when he gets home that will be another story." Sarah announced as she sat down beside Eilish.

A collective sigh spread through the group as they heard this news. They exchanged glances and obvious gestures, all conveying their shared sense of relief.

"Thank God," Said Alison, "When does he get out of there?"

"They are not sure yet but hopefully by the end of the week."

Everyone took a minute to process the good news but then reality set in about the present moment of Andrew and his cronies.

Brian paced the small living room, running a hand through his hair. "We should've heard something on the news by now, right? It's 24 hours."

Alison snorted. "Aye, or it means they're burying the evidence as we speak."

"Don't even joke about that," Eilish snapped, immediately regretting her tone. "Sorry, I'm just... on edge."

A news anchor's solemn face filled the frame. Still nothing about Callum or the tanker.

Eilish glanced at the others. "What if the police drag their feet, or worse...Alison is right. I mean the longer they are free the more danger Callum is in, sorry Sarah but you know it's what we are all thinking."

Brodie nodded then blurted out. "The Oban Times. If we go public, there's no burying this."

"It's risky," Brian warned, but his eyes said it was a great idea. "We'll be painting targets on our backs."

"Maybe, but maybe not if we stay anonymous and journalists usually don't reveal their sources, we probably should have done that in the first place." Eilish stated.

"Then let's move," Alison said, grabbing her keys. "I know the editor, he'll listen."

They piled into Alison's battered Land Rover, the tires kicking up gravel as they sped towards town. Everyone's mind going a mile a minute, rehearsing what to say, what to emphasize. The weight of the evidence in the bag felt like an anchor.

"What if they don't believe us?" Eilish whispered to Brian.

He squeezed her shoulder. "They will. We've got proof, remember?"

"I know, but still," Eilish muttered, her confidence fading.

The newspaper office loomed ahead, a lone light burning in an upstairs window. Alison killed the engine.

"Right," she said, her voice steely. "Let's make some noise."

Inside, they cornered the night editor, a weary-looking man named Duncan. Brian spread out their documents, his voice steady as he outlined the corruption, the cover-up, Callum's trauma.

Duncan's eyes widened. "Christ almighty," he breathed. "This is... huge."

"It needs to run," Brodie insisted. "First thing tomorrow."

Duncan nodded, already reaching for his phone. "I'm calling in the whole team. This is front page material, but I can't do tomorrow, I'm sorry lads."

Brodie, jumped in, "What do you mean, why not?"

Duncan still scanning the pages of shocking proof, looked up and said, "That's not how it's done, I can't just throw all this on the front page without checking sources, facts, if this isn't true it would finish me. Look I have a first-rate team with connections all over the place, give me, at the most, forty-eight hours, that's all I ask?"

The group looked at each other, I suppose it was too much to ask to put such big news up without him wanting to fact check.

Brian said to Duncan, "Give us a sec, would you?"

"Sure," Both parties understanding the others plight.

Brian waved everyone to the other side of the room.

Brodie broke the silence, "What do ye want to do? I say no way what if he is connected to Andrew?"

Eilish agreed, "Exactly he could be setting us up too, giving Andrew more time and get us killed."

Alison and Jan almost spoke at the same time.

Alison was a second ahead of Jan, "No, I have known Duncan for years, he is good friends with my dad, he is a good man, he is just doing his Job."

Jan right behind Alison, announces while staring at Duncan behind his desk, "He is okay."

Brodie, Brian and Eilish look at each other, Brodie throws up his arms.

"Okay then, let's do this."

They go back to Duncan, essentially putting their lives in his hands.

Alison says, "Go on Duncan, get it up when ye can, alright."

Duncan now sitting at his desk picks up the phone and gets to work.

Eilish sagged against Brian, exhaustion but relief washing over her.

"We did it," she murmured.

"Not yet," he reminded her gently. "But we're close."

The next forty-eight hours seemed like forever, but then the story broke, dominating headlines across Scotland. Eilish watched, stunned, as the consequences unfolded with dizzying speed.

Police raids on the oil company offices and Mabel's office. Executives led away in handcuffs. Andrew and Mabel brought in for questioning. Share prices plummeting.

"I can't believe it," Eilish whispered, staring at the TV in Alison's living room. "It's actually happening."

As the dust began to settle, Eilish felt a weight lift from her shoulders. They'd done it. They'd exposed the truth, consequences be damned.

She caught Brian's eye and saw her own unspoken thoughts reflected there: Pure relief.

Eilish's phone buzzed with a news alert, she swiped it open, her breath catching.

"Guys," she called, her voice trembling. "Look at this."

Sarah, Jan, Brodie and Brian crowded around her, peering at the screen. The headline blazed: Scottish Parliament Announces Sweeping Environmental Protections for Isle of Mull.

Brian's eyes widened. "Bloody hell, that was fast."

Eilish skimmed the article, her heart racing. "They're implementing strict regulations on industrial activity near the coastline. Enhanced protections for marine life. Increased funding for conservation efforts."

Sarah squeezed her shoulder. "Well done, all of you. Well guess where I'm off too?" her voice was way too cheery for them not to figure it out.

Brian said it first, "You're not? Is he coming home today?"

Sarah grinned from ear to ear.

"Feck off," said Brodie with a big smile, "Oh so now the real pain begins, isn't that right Sarah?"

Sarah shoved Brodie's shoulder, "Shut up, Brodie," with a tear in her eye.

Brodie held out his arms, Sarah embraced him crying. Everyone felt what she was feeling, this nightmare was coming to an end.

Brian came up behind Eilish and pulled her in close, this was a moment that needed to be remembered and cherished. For Callum's recovery, for what they had achieved and for what was to come. How often do you have a group of people in your life you can trust with everything you have? As Sarah went out the door, Brodie turned quickly away pretending to look out the window, but the slight occasional sniffle gave him away.

~

It was time for Eilish and Brian to head back to Florida.

They stepped out into the brisk Mull air. It was time to part ways with Jan. Both Eilish and Brian found it hard to lift their embrace from this amazing woman. Eilish had never met anyone like her before and knew she never would. Eilish moved away to let Brian say his own goodbyes. Eddie was waiting with his red truck to bring them and their bags to the ferry.

As Eilish stepped into the truck, a flash of movement caught her eye. A seal, dark and sleek, bobbed in the choppy waves. She felt an inexplicable pull towards the water.

Although it was a lengthy voyage home, they didn't mind. After all, the excitement and tension they had just experienced, simply sitting on a train and then a plane with nothing else to do but be next to each other was comforting and satisfying. There were no complaints from either of them.

Thank you

Dear readers

Thank you sincerely for reading my book. As a first-time author, your time and interest in my book mean a great deal to me. Sharing the journey of Brian and Eilish with you has been an incredible experience.

If you have a moment, I would greatly appreciate your honest feedback on Amazon. Your reviews not only help others discover the book, but also allow me to learn about your personal experiences with the story.

This will take you to the review page on amazon.
Kind regards
Sierra